OTHER BOOKS BY FELICIA DONOVAN

The Black Widow Agency

FORTHCOMING BOOKS BY FELICIA DONOVAN

Fragile Webs

Spun
TALES

felicia donovan

MIDNIGHT INK
WOODBURY, MINNESOTA

FIRST EDITION
First Printing, 2008

Based on book design by Rebecca Zins
Book format by Donna Burch
Cover design by Ellen Dahl
Cover image © Colin Anderson/Blend Images/PunchStock
Editing by Connie Hill

Midnight Ink, an imprint of Llewellyn Publications

Cover model(s) used for illustrative purposes only
and may not endorse or represent the book's subject.

Library of Congress Cataloging-in-Publication Data

Donovan, Felicia.
   Spun tales / Felicia Donovan. —1st ed.
      p. cm. — (The Black Widow Agency ; #2)
   ISBN: 978-0-7387-1310-6 (alk. paper)
   1. Women private investigators—Fiction. 2. Electronic surveillance—Fiction.
3. Chick lit. I. Title.

PS3604.O5667S78   2008
813'.6—dc22   2008002830

Midnight Ink
2143 Wooddale Drive, Dept. 978-0-7387-1310-6
Woodbury, MN 55125-2989

www.midnightinkbooks.com

Printed in the United States of America

ACKNOWLEDGMENTS

To my parents, Sharon and Rolph, for all their love and support.

To my agent, Jill Grosjean, who continues to believe.

*To the folks at Midnight Ink books, many thanks
to everyone for a job well done.*

And always, to Jess and John, with all my love.

"READY, ALEX?" KATIE MAHONEY asked Alexandria Axelrod as she handed her a black leather briefcase. Alexandria nodded. "You're sure about this?" Katie asked with some hesitation. "You know you don't have to do it. I can just tail him all the way."

"It's fine."

"And the bailout word is?"

"Chocolate."

"If either of us has any problems, or even if something doesn't feel right, that's the emergency word. And if either of us has any emergency cravings, that's the solution," Katie added, laughing.

Alexandria gazed at her vacantly.

"Remember, the only thing I need is the room number," Katie said as she glanced out the one-way window toward the street. A heavyset, middle-aged man with gray hair and thick, tortoise-shelled glasses suddenly came into view.

"Okay, it's showtime."

Katie pointed the video camera out the window of the white van that had "Divinity Florals" painted on its side. "That's him," she said pointing, "navy-blue suit, white shirt, floral tie, gray hair, coke-bottom glasses." She motioned Alexandria to come over so she could see her target. Without thinking, Katie touched Alexandria's elbow to pull her closer. Alexandria immediately recoiled.

"Sorry," Katie said casually. "You see him?" Alexandria nodded. "Wait … wait … okay, go."

Katie sat back and watched as Alexandria, with her long legs and wide stride, easily caught up to the man and fell into step behind him as he approached the entrance to the Constitution Hotel on Bolton Avenue. This was a routine case—although she knew from her years as a police officer that there was danger in letting one's guard down and feeling complacent. Still, all the wife wanted was the incriminating evidence before she filed for divorce and, so far, it had been an easy case to work—the husband having enjoyed the company of one of the new assistants routinely every Tuesday at two p.m. All they needed now was the video to finalize the case and they could wrap things up and start on the next one.

BUSINESS WAS BOOMING AT the Black Widow Agency, where disgruntled wives and girlfriends hired Katie and her co-workers to get the goods on their errant husbands and boyfriends. When they weren't in the field using the latest covert video surveillance cameras, they were back at the offices using the latest computer forensic software to digitally analyze amorous e-mails, recover deleted e-mail orders for flowers and trinkets, and uncover undisclosed bank accounts. It was hard work and long hours, but the women of the agency, all of whom had been scorned in one way or another by a man, were more than up for the task, especially if it meant helping a woman in need.

Katie swiveled in the mounted chair and switched to the remote cameras and microphones located in the briefcase Alexandria was carrying. She watched and listened on her headset as Alexandria, without giving the man so much as a glance, stepped into the elevator behind him. He turned around and politely asked her what floor she needed him to press. Alexandria deliberately fumbled around in her purse until she saw him press "six."

"Sixth floor, please," she said pulling out her cell phone and taking a few discrete pictures of the man while they rode up. As the elevator doors opened, the man stepped aside to let her exit first. Alexandria stepped out of the elevator and fumbled around again in her purse for a small compact. With her back to the man, she pretended to freshen up her lipstick. She pressed the small lid release in the front of the compact; a mini camera zoomed in, giving Alexandria a clear shot of the hallway directly behind her. She noted the door the man knocked on and could hear a woman's voice as it was opened. With her back still toward him, Alexandria captured the woman embracing the man and drawing him in. As soon as the door was shut, Alexandria removed her shoes, tiptoed down the hall, noted the room number, and headed down the stairwell.

Upon hearing three successive raps on the van's back door, Katie opened it and held out her hand to help Alexandria up, but

Alexandria ignored the gesture and grabbed onto the door to hoist herself up.

"Six-twenty-two," Alexandria announced as Katie jotted down the room number on a "Divinity Florals" receipt.

"Wish me luck," Katie said as she grabbed the gift basket that Margo Norton, their office manager, had assembled for them earlier. In it were Lindt chocolate truffles, a bottle of champagne, glasses, and some imported cheese and crackers. Woven throughout the basket were tiny remote buttonhole cameras disguised as the heads of flowers.

Katie pulled her "Divinity Florals" cap down low on her head and, without saying another word, hopped out the back of the van. She walked into the main lobby of the hotel with a confident stride, as if she went there every day. The concierge looked up briefly at her. Katie smiled and waved to the young man as if they'd met many times before, and held up the basket. He nodded toward her and waved back. Without a word, she stepped onto the elevator and rode up to the sixth floor.

She knocked on the door and waited.

"Who is it?" a man's voice called out.

"Delivery," she said loudly. She deliberately smiled at the peephole and held the basket up in front of her.

The man opened the door just a crack. His tie was off, his shirt was half-unbuttoned and his belt was loosened. Katie glanced behind him and saw a young woman on the bed, wrapped only in a hotel robe.

"Delivery," Katie said again and, without asking, tried to push past him and walk in.

The hefty man positioned himself in the door frame and put his arm out to stop her as he pushed his thick glasses back up on the bridge of his nose. "There must be some mistake," he said, "we didn't call for any delivery."

Katie frowned and showed him the receipt. "Constitution Hotel, room six-twenty-two." The man took the receipt from her and studied it.

"What is it, Saul?" the young woman sitting on the bed asked.

"I'll take care of it," he said, glancing nervously over his shoulder. He pointed to the receipt and showed Katie. "It says 'Harrington'," he said. "You must have the wrong person," he added as he handed her back the receipt.

Katie pretended to study the receipt more closely, then glanced at her watch.

"Oh shit. They must have already checked out. Damn!" she said, glancing nervously back and forth. "Look, I'm going to catch all kinds of crap if I bring this back to the shop," she said. "I was supposed to be here for this morning but that damned traffic ... Do me a favor, would you, and just keep it anyway, okay?"

"But we didn't—" the man started to say, but the young woman with the long, dark hair sauntered up behind him and placed her hand on his shoulder. She was half his age and not altogether attractive. Her nose was a bit too large for her face and her hair was a variation of colors from auburn at the roots to brunette at the tips, as if she couldn't quite decide what color she wanted it to be. She was well-endowed and the robe was open enough for Katie to see her biggest assets.

"Ooh, is that champagne?" the young woman asked in a nasal tone as she leaned closer. She slipped her arms around the man's waist and oozed out, "I wouldn't mind a little champagne before we…"

The man glanced nervously at Katie and back out the door. "Okay, whatever, we'll keep it."

Katie shoved past him and set the basket on the dresser directly in front of the bed. "You two have a real good time," she called out over her shoulder as she hurried back toward the elevator.

"LET'S SEE WHAT'S ON our favorite channel," Katie said as she took a seat in the back of the van. Alexandria was already at the console, monitoring several views from the cameras.

"That's the most expensive gift basket they'll ever get," Katie said, referring to the cost of the hidden cameras. The view was incredible. "Excellent video quality."

"Those are the VT-twenty-threes," Alexandria explained with some pride. "They have three hundred and eighty lines of resolution, a point-five low lux rating, the latest CMOS imager, and a built-in, three-point-five-millimeter lens with a sixty-degree field of view."

"Let's just hope his wife appreciates the fine quality of the video," Katie said as she watched the woman undo the man's belt.

"Looks like he has a sweet spot," Katie chuckled. Alexandria watched with no expression whatsoever on her face. "Or should I say," Katie corrected herself, "a sweet and low spot." She leaned back a bit as the sordid action began to unfold in front of her. A few minutes later, she commented, "If that's him all worked up, it sure doesn't look like there's much to work with." Katie rocked the chair back and forth and the two women watched in silence for several minutes.

"Is it just me," Alexandria said after a few minutes, "or does it look like he's swaying?"

Just as she uttered the words, they watched on the monitors as the man slumped forward on top of the young woman, his body weight forcing her back onto the bed. Katie and Alexandria glanced at each other for a second in disbelief, then back to the monitor as they watched the young woman struggle to climb out from under the collapsed body.

"Oh, boy," Katie said as she grabbed her cell phone and dialed the office of the Black Widow Agency.

"What are you doing?" Alexandria asked.

Margo Norton answered the phone immediately. "Hey, Margo, it's Katie."

"How's the action?" Margo asked. "You learning anything new, Girlfriend?"

"Yeah, that sex can kill."

"Huh?"

"Listen, I need you to get on an untraceable line right away and call 9-1-1 for a possible heart attack at the Constitution Hotel, room six-twenty-two. Got that?"

"Constitution Hotel, room six-twenty-two," Margo repeated back. "Got it."

They continued to watch the video monitor as the young woman finally managed to extricate herself from underneath the body. She shook the man repeatedly and called his name. He didn't move. The young woman picked up the hotel phone, held it in the air for a second, then quickly set it back down.

Katie and Alexandria watched in shock as the young woman gathered up her clothes, slipped her dress back on, and stole out of the room, leaving her fallen lover to fend for himself.

"Nice," Katie said, shaking her head. "Must be true love." She nodded toward Alexandria. "Okay, let's go," she said.

"Go where?" Alexandria asked.

"We can't just leave him there. Let's go."

"But our cover…"

"Isn't going to matter one bit if he's dead," Katie replied. "There's light coming from the hallway, so she probably left the door open when she took off. Come on."

"What are we supposed to do?" Alexandria asked with a small edge to her voice.

"Well, we can't just leave him there to die," Katie said. "Come on, Alex, seconds count."

"But we…"

"Now!" Katie said more firmly. Without waiting, Katie jumped out of the back of the van and walked quickly toward the entrance to the hotel. Neither woman said a word as they walked into the hotel lobby and past the Concierge's desk.

"Busy morning?" the concierge said in a friendly tone.

"Beats a dead morning," Katie threw back as they entered the elevator. At the room, the door was slightly ajar. The man's body was pitched forward, half slumped on the bed, with his upper body on the mattress and his lower body sagging toward the floor. Katie thought it looked a little like he was praying. *He'd better be*, she thought to herself.

"Alright, Alex, here's what we're going to do," she said very calmly. "I'm going to pull his head and shoulders back and you're going to take his legs and straighten them out so we can get him flat on the floor on his back." Katie straddled the man's body from around his back and grabbed him under the shoulders and pulled. Alexandria stood nearby, motionless.

"Now would be a good time to help, Alex," Katie said, with more than a tad of sarcasm in her voice. "Like right now," she said again as the full weight of the man's body pushed back against her and forced her back into the dresser. Alexandria came forward very reluctantly and with a disgusted expression, grabbed the man's legs and pulled them. Both women struggled to pull the dead weight of the man around. Katie immediately knelt down beside him and felt for a pulse. When she couldn't find one, she bent her head down to his exposed chest and listened.

"Do you know CPR?" she asked Alexandria as she straddled the man's body and felt for the location of his sternum.

"No … I couldn't," Alexandria answered.

"Come on," Katie said in between thrusts to the man's chest. "Start blowing."

Alexandria's eyes grew wide. "I … I can't."

Katie glanced at her rather sharply. "He's not breathing, Alex, come on. Just lift his chin up, clear his airway, put your mouth on his, and blow," Katie said.

Alexandria knelt down very slowly. She brushed away her short, black hair and got close to the man's face.

"Seconds count, Alex."

Alexandria started to bend down toward the man's mouth, but backed away. "I can't," she said quietly.

"You have to," Katie said in between thrusts. "He could suffer brain damage if you don't. Come on, Alex, you can do this."

Again, Alexandria bent forward, got close to the man's mouth, and again she immediately sat upright.

"I … I just can't," she said.

Katie shook her head. "If you can't do this, then for God's sake go find me someone who can."

Alexandria watched for a few seconds as Katie shifted her position, lifted the man's neck with the heel of her hand and arched his head back. Katie covered the man's mouth with hers and breathed in very slowly, checking to see that his chest was rising. She looked up for a second. "Damn it, if he has some disease or something, I'll kill him myself," she said.

With that, Alexandria walked out.

After a few minutes of alternating between rescue breathing and compressions, Katie was beginning to wonder how much longer she could last. Her muscles were tiring, her back ached, and she felt slightly dizzy and short of breath. After one more set of breaths, she noticed a small rise in the man's chest followed by a slight movement in his arm. She stopped and felt a weak pulse. He at least appeared to be breathing on his own again. She kept a finger on his carotid pulse as the ambulance crew and the hotel security officer showed up.

"Cardiac arrest," she told them. "He's been out for approximately six minutes and I've been doing CPR for the last four. Subject's name is Saul Levine and he's probably got ID on him in his wallet."

The EMTs knelt down and relieved Katie of her duties as they started hooking him up to a portable EKG machine.

"Are you related?" one of them asked.

"No."

"Staying with him?"

"No. I was just here to make a delivery," she said as she pulled herself up. Katie quickly grabbed the gift basket before anyone else could ask her any more questions and bolted out the door. She saw Alexandria standing by the elevator with her back turned. Ignoring her completely, Katie pressed the down button. As the elevator doors opened up, she saw two blue uniforms. She quickly jerked her baseball cap way down and held the basket up to obscure her face. The last thing she wanted was to be recognized by one of her former fellow officers and have to explain what she was doing there. Alexandria got on the elevator behind her and they rode down in silence. Neither spoke until Katie got behind the wheel and announced, "I need a drink." Alexandria said nothing.

Katie pulled into The Blue Line, the bar owned by her former partner Sean McCleary.

"Katie, my girl, how are you?" Sean McCleary yelled as he waved to her. Sean's once-red hair was now mostly gray but his eyebrows were still distinctively red and bushy.

"Pissier than thirsty and too thirsty to piss," she answered back sharply. Cocking her thumb back over her shoulder she said, "This is Alexandria."

"A pleasure," Sean said extending his hand, but Alexandria just stood there.

"She doesn't like to touch or be touched," Katie announced rather loudly, glaring at Alexandria as if to dare her to say anything.

Sean looked curiously at the tall, thin woman and pulled his hand back. "So what can I get for you ladies?" he asked.

"I'll have a Smuttynose Ale," Katie replied.

Sean looked at her curiously. "Have you given up your beloved scotch entirely, Katie?" he asked.

"This is my version of a health-food kick," Katie said. "Less alcohol, more water."

"I see," Sean said as he pulled from the tap. "And for you?" he said nodding toward Alexandria.

"Diet soda, please," Alexandria said quietly. Katie rolled her eyes.

Sean placed their drinks on the bar and Katie grabbed them up and gestured toward a booth. It was early and the Blue Line was nearly empty.

Katie knocked back a good portion of her beer and set the glass down loudly on the table. Alexandria jumped slightly.

"Tell me one thing, Alex," Katie began, "let's say that had been me back there. Let's say I keeled over and wasn't breathing. Would you have helped me?"

"Of course."

"How?" Katie asked.

"I would have gotten you help," Alexandria answered.

"What if I needed CPR? What if I choked right now and needed the Heimlich?"

"Do you need the Heimlich right now?" Alexandria asked.

Katie picked the glass back up and finished off the rest of the beer. Sean looked over, but she waved him off.

"I don't understand, Alex," Katie began. "I just don't get it."

"What don't you get?"

"You. This thing. This aversion to being touched." Katie deliberately reached across the table as she said the words and put her hand on Alexandria's arm. Alexandria immediately pulled back.

"He could have died, Alex."

"But he didn't. You saved his life. Your being there made the difference."

"But what if I hadn't been there?" Katie asked. "What if it had been me in trouble. Or Margo? Or Jane? Geez, Jane could go any minute with all those hot flashes she's having. God only knows how screwed up her body is right now. Would you have just stood by and said, 'Sorry, I can't help because I don't like to touch people?'"

"He didn't die, Katie."

"Alex, all I'm saying is that you're missing out on a lot of life because of this ... this thing you have. Maybe it's time you talked to someone about it. Maybe someone could help you work through this and figure out the reason."

"What makes you think I don't know the reason?"

A FEW WEEKS LATER, Katie Mahoney sat and watched a tall, middle-aged man, with a full head of brown hair, and a young, heavily endowed woman board a boat docked several slips away.

"Look at that WOMB," Margo commented, using their standard acronym for "Women Of Mighty Breasts." "If that girl goes overboard, she'll be floating face up, that's for damn sure."

Katie laughed and glanced at the boat's name, *The Two of Us*. "How ironic is that?" she said. "It would be more accurate if it was *The TOW of Us*," Katie observed, using their slang for "The Other Woman."

Katie grabbed her compact from her bag and turned her back to *The Two of Us*. Pressing the release lid on the side, she zoomed the lens of the hidden digital video camera and checked the display on the laptop to make sure everything was being recorded. The picture was incredibly sharp.

"I wonder which half of the boat the wife will want," she said as she taped them for a few minutes. She paused and glanced anxiously at her watch. "You're sure they're coming?"

"I told them ten a.m. In Marcus' time, that means ten thirty and not a minute sooner," Margo said, referring to her twin brother.

Katie watched as another, much newer-looking boat pulled out a few slips away from them. Katie noted the boat's name, *The End,* along with the middle-aged woman, small in stature with red hair, wearing a wide-brimmed, bright blue straw hat and dark sunglasses, at the helm. A flash of light gleamed from around the woman's neck as the sun reflected off what Katie assumed was a necklace. Even with the hat pulled down and the sunglasses on, there was something vaguely familiar about her profile. A glint of light flashed again as the woman turned the wheel.

"Do you know who that is?" Katie asked, nodding toward the boat.

"How the hell should I know?" Margo answered. "I didn't get this dark skin from sitting around on a boat all my life."

Katie grabbed her cell phone. "Hey Janie, how are you? Really? And what did little MaryJane say today?" Katie said rolling her eyes at Margo. "That granddaughter of yours sure is a smartie. Listen, can you put me through to Alex? She's not? Do you know where she went? I see..." Katie shook her head and sighed. "When she gets back, can you have her run a marine registration for me on a boat called, *The End*? Thanks. I'll look at the new pictures of Mary-Jane when we get back, okay?"

Katie shut the phone and shook her head. "You'll be shocked to know she has new pictures of her granddaughter. Oh yeah, and today she said, 'Wee-we-ell.'"

15

"Huh?"

"I guess it means cereal. I don't know. I'm just so sick of hearing about little MaryJane every freaking day of my life. MaryJane crawled on her own across the floor. MaryJane is cutting her third tooth."

"So where's Miss Anorexia today?"

"Not in the office, and I wish you wouldn't call her that."

"Let me guess. Miss Skin and Bones has done a disappearing act again."

"Apparently, but really, Margo, I don't think it's necessary…"

"You sure she didn't just turn sideways somewhere?" Margo said as she pretended to glance around the boat.

Katie tapped her fingernails on the helm of the boat impatiently. "Enough, Margo."

"Did you ever think of asking her where she goes?"

"I have."

"And?"

"She says it's personal."

"How personal?"

"I don't know."

"You don't suppose…"

"Suppose what, Margo?"

"You know damn well what, Katie, that maybe she's got some cyber lover stashed away somewhere and she meets him for a little… you know… digital penetration?" Margo said, her brown eyes flashing.

"Alex? Our Alex?"

"He might have a really big hard drive…"

"If she does, I guess it's her business."

"Oh come on, Katie. Don't pull that "it's her business" crap with me. It must be damn near killing you."

"What are you talking about?" Katie asked, slightly annoyed.

"You know how it bugs you to not be able to figure something out. Here you are, Katie Mahoney, the Great White Detective, and you don't have a clue where your own Geek Goddess disappears to all the time. Must drive you crazy."

Katie glared at Margo for a minute. "Fine. If you must know, it does bother me, but you know how Alex is. She lives in her own little world. Frankly, I'd be hugely relieved to find she had a guy stashed somewhere instead of . . ."

"Instead of what?"

"Never mind . . ."

IT HAD BEEN SEVERAL years since Katie Mahoney, ex-police detective, had stumbled upon a scheme whereby a young hacker, Alexandria Axelrod, was stealing money from huge corporations. Unlike most thieves, the stolen money had all been donated to various charities. It had remained a mystery to Katie, even after she arrested Alexandria, why this young Cyber Robin Hood, now her co-worker and computer forensics examiner, never used any of the money for her own gain.

KATIE'S CELL PHONE BEGAN to hum the theme to "Charlie's Angels," prompting Margo to roll her eyes. Katie stuck her tongue out at her and grabbed the phone.

"Hey Alex. How are you? They are? Can't this state ever buy computers that don't crash every two minutes? Okay, keep trying and let me know if you get it. Oh, and Alex? How's your morning going? I'm just asking that's all. Do anything exciting? Okay, well, I guess I'll be talking to you then." Katie flipped the cover over on the phone and jammed it into her pocket.

"Nice try," Margo said.

Katie looked over and saw that the man and woman aboard *The Two of Us* were still busy loading bottles of wine on board.

"Guess they're planning a party. Probably charged to an expense account, too." Katie looked over again at *The End*.

"Why do you want to know who owns that boat when it's not the one we're watching?" Margo asked.

Katie watched as *The End* pulled away from the marina. "I don't know. There's just something familiar about her profile."

"Girl, you say that all the time."

Glancing at her watch, Katie said, "You're positive they're coming, right?"

"I just told you...," Margo began, but just as she did, two black men—one tall and slim in tan shorts and a tank top, the other much shorter and stouter in flowing lavender silk pants and a flowering shirt with a bottle of champagne tucked under his arm—came into view, walking hand-in-hand down the pier.

"Yoo-hoo!" Marcus waved. "Yoo-hoo!"

"So much for being low-key," Katie moaned.

"Katie, you're on a damn boat named *The FlameBoyant*, with lavender flags flying and Marcus on board. How low-key did you think we were gonna be?"

"I see your point."

"We're here, Black Widows!" Marcus yelled out as Antoine stepped aboard and held out a hand for his partner.

"Hey Marcus," Katie said as he came aboard, "This is a covert surveillance. You know, undercover operation."

"Oooh," Marcus replied. "I like being under covers," he said as he squeezed Antoine's shoulders.

"Marcus," his sister began, "why don't you turn the dial down on your queer-a-meter a few notches, okay? This is a big case and we don't want our cover blown."

"Another thing I like to do," Marcus said with a gleam in his eye. His sister smacked him on the shoulder, nearly sending the bottle of champagne to the floor. "Ow!"

"Well, you deserved it."

"Look, they're ready to roll," Katie said as *The Two of Us* began to back out of its slip. "Can we get started up?"

"Underway," Marcus corrected her.

"Huh?"

"On a boat, you get underway, not get started up, Katarina darling."

"So what's the game plan?" Antoine asked as he began his safety check.

"See that boat three slots down with the blue awning pulling out?"

"That's 'slips' and it's called a 'canopy' and they're 'getting underway,'" Marcus corrected her.

Katie rolled her eyes. "Whatever …"

"I see it."

"We go when they go, but discreetly."

"Looks like they're getting ready to shove off," Antoine said.

Marcus looked over at the boat and the scantily clad woman in the hot pink bikini with cleavage spilling out. "Polly Darton, she looks buoyant."

"Like I said," Margo added, "that girl's guaranteed to float with those silicone surfboards."

The woman wrapped her arms around the man's waist as the boat moved out.

"Okay, so let's go ... I mean get underway, whatever," Katie said, thinking the whole idea of going with Marcus and Antoine may have been a big mistake. Trustworthy they were. Low-key, Marcus was not.

"Aye-aye, Captain," Antoine said.

Marcus came up from behind him and squeezed his arm. "Ooh, I just love it when he does his nautical talk. Floats my boat, if you get what I mean."

"I get it," Katie said.

"Champagne, Katarina darling?" Marcus asked popping the cork on the bottle.

"I'm all set. Margo, make a note that the boat left the slot ... I mean the slip ...," she paused to check her watch, "at ten-thirty-eight."

Antoine waited for the other boat to depart before throwing the engine in reverse and slowly easing *The FlameBoyant* out of its slip. He throttled forward slowly, keeping plenty of distance between the two vessels.

"How much distance do you want between us and them?" Antoine asked. "He's got a pair of pretty powerful twins."

"I have to disagree, darling," Marcus interrupted, "You mean she's got a set of powerful twins. Those things could be lethal.

Speaking of powerful twins …," Marcus said, nudging his twin sister, Margo, but she was too busy clutching the seat with her hands to respond. Marcus sipped on his champagne and gestured with his glass toward Antoine. "He can handle this powerful twin anytime," he said. Antoine smiled.

KATIE PULLED OUT A ruggedized laptop with a fully sealed aluminum alloy case that could withstand a bullet or complete submersion—or, more likely, a spilled cup of coffee. The screen came to life and Antoine looked at a nautical map that showed a small red circle and a green triangle that both blinked and moved.

"I got here early and hid an AVL, an Automatic Vehicle Locator, on their boat," Katie explained. "They're the red target. This laptop has built-in GPS, so we're green. Even if we lose sight of them, we'll still be able to figure out where they are."

"How high-tech," Antoine observed.

The FlameBoyant moved slowly until reaching the open waters. Antoine engaged the engines as soon as they cleared the channel. Katie tilted her head back and enjoyed the feeling of sea spray on her face.

"So Antoine, where did you learn about boats?"

"Courtesy of the U.S. Navy."

Katie dropped her sunglasses down on her nose and looked at him. "You … you were in the Navy?" she asked.

"It was during the don't ask, don't tell days."

"I see."

"That's right, Katarina, darling," Marcus said proudly. "My beloved Antoine was in the Navy. You know what that makes him, don't you? A seaman," Marcus said, licking the lip of his glass.

"Marcus, behave," Margo said.

"And he knows the difference between the porthole and the head," Marcus added, as his sister reached across and swatted him on the shoulder.

"Stop hitting me!" Marcus said.

"Then stop being a damn jerk!" Margo said.

"Okay, you know what?" Katie interrupted. "We're really not supposed to be drawing attention to ourselves, so if you two want to have a family domestic, why don't you take it downstairs."

"That's below decks," Marcus corrected her.

"He does it on purpose," Margo said. "Marcus loves to draw attention to himself. Always has."

"She's delirious from the sun," Marcus replied gesturing at his sister with his glass.

"He sued our high school to be able to go to the prom with Warren Johnson. Believe me, I was lucky any guy would date me after that."

Katie couldn't help but smile.

"And damn if he didn't look better in his gown than I did in mine."

"I had the hips," Marcus explained. "So tell me, Katarina darling, why are we on this super secret mission?"

Katie gestured toward *The Two of Us*.

"Because that man, Mr. Big Executive, told his wife he was going on a business trip to Kansas for three days."

"Oh dear, Toto, I don't think we're in Kansas anymore."

"No, and he can click his heels all he wants, but she's still going to get their two-million-dollar home and half that boat."

They got farther and farther from shore. Katie enjoyed the gentle roll of the boat as it went through the open water. Marcus sipped eagerly at his champagne. Margo dug her nails deeper and deeper into the seat cushion.

"Are you okay, Margo?" she asked.

"I . . . I think so."

The FlameBoyant suddenly slowed down.

"It looks like they're going to drift for a bit," Antoine said. "We'll just drift here as well."

"Shouldn't we put out an anchor or something?" Katie asked.

"Set the anchor," Marcus corrected her. "You set the anchor."

"Whatever."

"If we do," Antoine explained, "it will take too long to bring it up if they get underway again. We're better off just drifting. Wherever the current takes them, we'll go, too."

Katie looked around and saw the other boat, *The End,* not too far off. The woman had moved to the back of the boat, and sat on the cushions with her feet propped up, typing away on a laptop. The glint of the silver necklace around her neck flashed like a beacon whenever the sun hit it. With her wide-brimmed, blue straw hat and sunglasses, Katie could not make out specific details of her face—still there was something familiar about her profile.

KATIE GLANCED OVER AT Margo and noticed her head was lowered and she was swallowing repeatedly.

"Margo, are you sure you're okay?" Katie asked.

"I … I don't know. I think maybe I'm going to …," Margo said as she abruptly leaned over the railing.

"Good god," Marcus said. "Why in heaven's name did you bring her along? My sister gets nauseous watching me stir a cocktail."

Antoine reached under and handed Katie some clean towels. Katie waited until Margo was done and handed one to her. "Marcus," she said, "take her downstairs … I mean below decks … to the bathroom …"

"The head," Marcus corrected her, "one of my favorite rooms. And you thought I was drawing attention to us," Marcus said. "I'm not the one doing the heave-ho over the side rails."

Margo was hunched over, holding her stomach.

"Please, Marcus," Katie said. "Just take care of your sister."

"Fine, but hold your studded stallions," Marcus said as he got up and helped his sister below decks.

KATIE SURREPTITIOUSLY RECORDED THE action as the man aboard *The Two of Us* threw his arm around the woman and gave her a long, passionate kiss. She kept recording as he worked his way down the woman's neck, as his hands undid the hook of her bikini, spilling her ample breasts out.

"Obviously fake," Antoine said, watching the screen.

Katie continued to record the sordid action for several more minutes, until the man finally took the woman's hand and led her below decks.

"If the boat's a rockin' …," Antoine said as he swiveled his seat and stretched his long legs out over the side.

KATIE SCANNED THE WATER. Her attention was suddenly drawn to a black boat in the distance, long and sleek, that seemed to come out of nowhere and was moving very fast toward the three boats that were all drifting freely in the currents. The front of the fast boat planed high out of the water, leaving only the stern to skim along the water's surface like a skipping stone bouncing along.

"Is that one of those cigar boats?" she asked.

"Cigarette."

"It's flying."

Antoine frowned. "It sure is and if he doesn't slow down, we're all going to get tossed from its wake. Idiot," Antoine muttered as he stood up and watched the approaching boat.

In the distance, Katie made out a single, male figure aboard the fast-moving boat, dressed in a black scuba suit with a hood. The boat continued on its course. Antoine started up the engine.

"What are you doing?" she asked.

"I'm getting ready when that wake hits. At the rate he's going, we may have to steer into it to keep from getting tossed aside. If that fool doesn't slow down, he's going to kill someone."

Katie watched as the woman aboard *The End*, who was typing on a laptop, suddenly looked up to see the fast-moving boat heading her way, reached around her neck, removed the necklace with the large silver fob and turned away from Katie before wrapping the fob back around her neck and quickly leaping to her feet. She raced to the helm and started up the engines of *The End*. Katie swung around with the makeup compact and began recording the action.

"She's thinking the same thing," Antoine said as he watched the cigarette boat come closer. "What is wrong with this guy?" he asked.

The man and woman aboard *The Two of Us* were nowhere to be seen. Katie had a pretty good idea what action below decks was keeping them so oblivious to all the action above decks.

Katie took the makeup compact and zoomed in on the woman's face just as she realized that the cigarette boat appeared to be bearing down straight toward *The End*.

"Dear Mercy," Antoine said quietly.

"Holy shit," Katie said as she finally got a very clear view of the woman's face.

THEY BOTH WATCHED TRANSFIXED as the large cigarette boat raced toward *The End*. Antoine waved his arms frantically, trying to get it to slow down, but the man in the black scuba suit stared straight ahead and continued on course.

Katie zoomed out to get a full picture of the action as the boat got closer and closer. Antoine quickly reached below, took out a small case and loaded a flare gun that he fired across the bow of *The FlameBoyant* toward the cigarette boat, trying to get the operator's attention. The woman on board *The End* looked up as the flare rose up and hung in the air.

Both Antoine and Katie watched as the woman threw her boat into full throttle and tried desperately to put distance between hers and the other boat, but as she turned, so did it. Within seconds, the two boats would collide.

They watched in dreadful anticipation for the impact. Katie dug her hands deep into the seat cushion and said the first prayer she could think of, *The Hail Mary*, for the woman, who had since stopped her boat and turned to face the oncoming boat, in what, resignation? A challenge? Defiance? Katie wasn't quite sure, but the woman remained perfectly still with her arms folded across her chest, her one hand cradling the silver rectangular fob around her neck and watched as the bow of the other boat came flying out of the water toward her.

Like something out of the movies, the boat launched high in the air and flew across the bow of *The End*. As it came crashing back down into the water, Katie was relieved to see the woman still standing on deck, unharmed. The black cigarette boat abruptly veered off and sped away, but the impact of the wake it left behind was so strong that *The End* rolled violently sideways and everything in it, including the woman, was tossed into the ocean.

The man and the woman aboard *The Two of Us* emerged, barely clothed, to see what was causing their boat to rock so violently. The man quickly went to the helm, started up the powerful twin engines and pulled away.

"Hang on!" Antoine shouted to Katie as he engaged the engines of *The FlameBoyant* to try and steer across the wall of water coming their way. The boat rocked end to end across the crest of the wave and it was all Katie could do to hang on to the back of the seat, trying desperately to recover her footing and not go sliding across the deck. They heard Marcus yell, "There goes my lovely drink!" as Antoine finally got control and began to steer the boat toward the woman. He cut the engines back and stripped off his tank top, but the boat rocked wildly from side to side as it bobbed across the wakes. *The End* had righted itself and was drifting away from them with no power.

"Come here," he said to Katie, gesturing her to the helm. "I need you to circle around while I pick her up, and then I'll swim toward you, okay?"

Before she could protest, Antoine slipped on a personal flotation device, grabbed a spare PFD that he wrapped around his arm, and dove into the water, swimming toward the woman who was trying desperately to stay afloat despite the powerful waves left by the other boat's wake. Katie could barely make out the blue straw hat, which was still miraculously tied to her head.

Katie grabbed the steering wheel and tried to circle around, but the force of the wake caused the boat to veer sharply to the left.

"And there's another glass gone!" Marcus shouted from below. "What is this, a twelve-step program?"

She ignored him and tried to put the boat back into a better course as she watched Antoine, who was an incredibly strong swimmer, work his way toward the woman, using the Australian crawl. For a few seconds, she lost sight of the woman as another wake covered her, but the bright blue hat bobbed back up in the water and Katie tried maneuvering closer. Just when she thought she saw her, the blue hat disappeared again. Antoine looked all around for the woman as Katie circled the boat toward him. Antoine must have spotted the woman, because he suddenly dove below the surface yet again. Katie watched anxiously for him to reappear and steered the boat toward where she'd seen him dive. After what seemed like minutes, but was really only seconds, she finally saw the blue hat emerge with Antoine holding an arm around the woman, directly in front of the boat's bow.

"Oh shit!" Katie yelled as she saw Antoine look up from trying to get the flotation vest around the woman to see his own boat bearing down on them. He clutched at the woman with one arm as he waved wildly at Katie.

"Bear off!" he screamed. "Bear off! Turn the wheel!"

Katie yanked hard at the wheel at the last second and the boat veered wildly to the right.

"That's it!" she heard Marcus scream from down below. "I demand a full refund for this trip!"

Katie glanced back, her heart in her mouth, to see Antoine giving her a thumbs up. She corrected the boat's position and brought it around again, but as she neared Antoine and the woman, she realized she didn't know how to make the boat stop.

"Where's the brake?" she yelled toward Antoine.

Antoine shook his head. "There is no brake," he yelled back.

"Well, how the hell am I supposed to stop this thing?" she yelled back.

"Put the throttle in neutral!"

She did and the boat suddenly slowed down and held its position.

"Keep it there," Antoine shouted as he swam toward the side. "Set the ladder on the transom." Katie could hear that he was out of breath.

"The what?"

"The trans... the side. Set the ladder on the side."

Katie found the small white ladder and hung it over the edge. She grabbed the arms of the woman and, with all her strength, hoisted her aboard as Antoine pushed her up the ladder from behind, and then climbed aboard himself.

"Are you okay?" she asked as they both collapsed into seats. The woman doubled over and was gasping for air and coughing.

Just then, Marcus appeared. "That's three good glasses of Moët …," Marcus began and stopped mid-sentence when he saw the woman. "Holy Mermaids," he said quietly as recognition set in.

"Find them some dry towels," Katie said. "Come on, Marcus," she said snapping her fingers.

Marcus opened up a bench seat and took out several dry towels with "S&S," for his and Antoine's interior design firm "Sachet and Sashay," monogrammed on them and handed them to Katie. They were thick, luxurious, and lavender. Katie tossed one to Antoine and wrapped the other one around the shivering woman's back. That's when she noticed the chain around her neck with the large silver-colored fob attached to it. It was rectangular, about the size of a cigarette lighter. The woman immediately reached to her chest and clutched at it. Katie heard her let out a huge sigh when she realized it was still there.

Just then, Antoine, who had been drying his hair with the towel, lowered the towel and looked at the woman he had just rescued, for the first time.

"You're …," he began to say.

"… Tired, cold, and exhausted, I'm sure," Katie interrupted. "Marcus, why don't you see if you or Margo can make some hot coffee for our guest."

Marcus continued to stare at the woman.

"Marcus? Did you hear me?" she said, snapping her fingers to get his attention. "Go make hot coffee."

"Actually, I'd prefer a cup of tea if it isn't too much trouble," the woman said in between shivers.

"Go!" Katie said as Marcus reluctantly went below decks.

THE WOMAN LEANED BACK against the seat cushion and shut her eyes. Antoine looked at Katie and raised his hands and shoulders, but Katie shrugged back.

A few minutes later, Marcus brought up a tray with hot tea, sugar, and lemon, followed by Margo, who stood wavering.

"It *is* her," Margo said, clutching the seat. Looking toward the water, she immediately clapped a hand over her mouth and went below again.

"Miss Jordan," Katie said, gently shaking the woman's shoulder, "we have some hot tea for you."

Linda Jordan's hands were shaking as she held the cup. She sipped the tea eagerly, and it seemed to do a lot to restore her.

"Thank you," she said, a tad stronger. "Thank you all, especially you," she said reaching toward Antoine. Antoine very gently took her hand in his and patted it.

"It's an honor, Miss Jordan," he said.

Just then, Katie's cell phone rang.

"Hello?"

"It's me," Alexandria said. "The state's computers just came back on line. Wait until I tell you who that boat is registered to."

"I think we already figured that out," Katie said.

"Well, do me a favor. If she falls in, let her go," Alexandria said, causing Katie to pull the phone away from her ear and stare at it for a second.

"What did you just say?"

"You heard me."

"You're too late," Katie said.

THE COAST GUARD INSISTED on interviewing each of them before they could be released. Linda Jordan's boat, *The End*, was towed back to port and the marine inspector was on his way to assess its seaworthiness, as was the insurance adjuster.

Margo was still quite unsteady on her feet and, for once, had little comment to make, having been below decks during all of the action.

Katie conveniently forgot to mention the video she had in her possession to anyone who interviewed her and prayed Antoine wouldn't say anything. Antoine's full statement didn't seem to overly impress the Coasties, given that he was an ex-Navy man. Marcus was the most animated, and went to great lengths to describe how three glasses of his best champagne had been spilled. It didn't take the Coast Guard long to realize he'd seen nothing. No one mentioned the real reason they were out on the water other than describing it as a "pleasure trip." Marcus and Antoine left together just before the press arrived in droves. Katie, Margo, and Linda Jordan were sent to the women's locker room to get dried off.

Linda Jordan shook her head. "Here we go," she said eyeing the swarm of reporters that were gathering in front of the Coast Guard station.

"I can help you with this," Katie assured her.

"Believe me, once they get you in their sights," Linda Jordan assured her, "they're ruthless. I guess I should get this over with," she said placing her hand on the well-polished doorknob.

Katie touched her arm. "Trust me, I have some experience with this kind of thing," Katie said as she grabbed her cell phone. "Just sit back down on this bench and wait a few minutes."

Linda Jordan looked at her curiously.

Ten minutes later, Jane arrived at the Coast Guard station dressed in a neatly ironed sleeveless white blouse and blue gabardine elastic-waist pants. Just as Katie had instructed her, she wore Katie's Red Sox cap walking in. She carried her oversized white purse under her arm.

"I got here as fast as I …," Jane began to say, but glancing at Linda Jordan, she dropped her purse to the floor. "You're … you're …," she stammered.

"Linda Jordan, meet Jane Landers."

"Miss Jordan," Jane said, pumping Linda Jordan's hand up and down, "this is such an honor."

"As you can see," Katie said, "we're all huge fans. Now Jane, did you make sure the reporters all saw you when you came in?"

"I made a point of asking why they were there, just like you said, Katie."

"Good. Now go into that ladies' room and take off what you're wearing."

"What?"

"You heard me. We need to get Miss Jordan out of here as quickly as possible, but we need a decoy."

"Oh, Katie, please … please don't make me do this again. I'm just an accountant."

"You're a valuable member of the team and you're the only one who can pull this off. Margo doesn't exactly fit the bill, if you know what I mean, and I'm too tall. You're the right height and body type. Now go in there and give us your clothes."

"But I've been wearing them … "

Linda Jordan interceded. "If it makes you feel any better, I've just taken a most unfortunate dunk in the ocean, so I'm not exactly clean myself."

Katie acted as the go-between as the two women swapped their clothes, including the wide-brimmed blue hat.

Jane stepped out of the booth.

"Perfect," Katie said. "Here's the plan … "

"I DON'T EVEN HAVE red hair," Jane protested.

"It doesn't matter. You're going to go out of here so quickly, they won't see your hair. We just need them to see the blue hat. We'll meet you back at the office."

"But how will I get away from them?" Jane asked nervously.

"Simple. Just take off your hat and your sunglasses and they'll figure it out. They're not that stupid. And make sure you're not followed."

"Katie, I wish you wouldn't make me do these things."

"Come on, Janie. You're an old, seasoned pro."

Jane began to fan herself. "Oh, dear," she said.

Katie rolled her eyes and grabbed a bunch of towels, wet them at the sink and handed them to her. "Hang in there, Janie, and use that power surge to our advantage, okay?"

KATIE GLANCED OVER AT Margo, who was sitting down, hugging the small bench. "Are you going to make it?"

"I feel like my upper GI just went to war against my lower GI."

"I'll drive," Katie said.

"Okay, Ladies, Operation Criss-Crossing Jordan is about to begin."

"If you ask me to synchronize anything, I'm gonna slap you," Margo said weakly.

"JANIE, IT'S ALL UP to you. Do your best to distract them. We'll be right behind you. And don't make eye contact with anyone. That goes for you, too, Miss Jordan," she said to Linda Jordan, who was now sporting Jane's clothes and Katie's Red Sox hat, "and act like you don't have a care in the world."

Jane Landers pulled the still wet blue straw hat down low on her head and stepped outside.

"IT'S HER!" KATIE HEARD rise up from the crowd of reporters as she slipped out the door of the Coast Guard Station. Jane walked quickly around the back as the throng of reporters gathered up their cameras and microphones and bolted after her.

"Okay, let's go," Katie said as she, Margo, and Linda Jordan walked casually out the front door.

They were almost to Katie's car when none other than Chelsea Mattox, local police-beat reporter and the woman Katie's ex-husband cheated on her with, came walking straight toward her. Katie picked up her pace, but Chelsea blocked her path.

"Well, well," Chelsea began. "What have we here? If it isn't the famous Black Widow Spider Women."

Katie gestured to Margo and Linda Jordan to keep moving.

"If you don't mind," Katie said as she tried to walk past her, but Chelsea continued to block her path.

"I do mind. Don't take me for a fool, Mahoney. If you're here, there's a lot more to this story."

Katie glanced around anxiously to make sure there were no other reporters in sight.

"Look," she began, "I know you'll never believe this, but I was working a completely unrelated job. It was purely coincidental that we were in the same place at the same time."

"Yeah, right," Chelsea said setting her hand on her ultra-thin hip bone. "Like I believe that." She flashed her coal-black eyes at Katie.

"I don't care if you believe me. I have a sick co-worker who needs to get home."

"Where is she?"

"She's probably puking in the car."

"You know who I mean."

"She just went around the back. Didn't you see?"

Chelsea Mattox looked around and spotted the two women in Katie's car.

"Who's that?" she asked.

"That's the team. We were all out here on surveillance."

Chelsea Mattox twisted her mouth around and stared at Katie's car. Katie glanced at her watch.

"As much as I love our little girlfriend chit-chats, Chelsea, I really do have to go. Now if you don't mind," she said as she tried to step forward. Chelsea Mattox grabbed Katie by the arm and pointed to the group of reporters who were eagerly chasing around the grounds after the woman they thought was Linda Jordan.

"You see those vultures?" she asked. "All I'd have to do is yell, 'She's here' and they'll swarm your car so badly, you'll never get out of here. Then they'll follow you back to your little spider web and your cover will be blown for good."

Katie studied the dark eyes and realized she was dead serious.

"What do you want?" Katie asked between gritted teeth.

"An exclusive."

"Not now," Katie said. "She's not in any shape."

"Fine, but within the week, she sits down and gives me an exclusive."

Katie shook her head. "You know, Chelsea, if only you'd put this much energy into doing something honorable, you might actually make something of yourself someday."

Chelsea Mattox gave Katie a smug look. "If I don't hear from you within the week, I'll write the story of my career, blowing your entire little spider operation."

Katie hesitated, knowing that an investigative agency's reputation was only as good as their ability to operate covertly. "Just to show I'm a fair person, I'll mention it to her."

"One week."

Katie pushed Chelsea's thin arm aside as she jumped into the front of her black SUV and drove off.

KATIE GLANCED IN THE rearview mirror. Linda Jordan looked pale.

"Miss Jordan?"

"Please, call me Linda."

"Very well. Linda, I don't quite know what happened out there on the water, but I have the feeling you're better off not going home right now."

"Yes," Linda answered weakly, "perhaps that would be best."

Katie watched as Linda fingered the chain around her neck and rubbed the silver fob several times.

"In that case, we have a very safe place for you to be until we figure this all out."

"Who ... who are you?" Linda asked curiously.

"We're the people who can keep you alive."

KATIE PULLED INTO THE Black Widow Agency's parking lot. She flipped open her cell phone and dialed Alex.

"Are we all clear?" she asked.

"Clear for what?"

"A guest. A very well-known guest."

Alexandria Axelrod zoomed the mounted cameras that had 360-degree views of their building, in on Katie's car.

"Tell me you're joking," she said.

"Ahhh … perhaps we can talk about this another time?" Katie said trying to be discrete. "Like as soon as our guest is settled in?"

"You know where to find me," Alexandria said before abruptly slamming the phone down.

KATIE GOT OUT OF her car, her trained eyes sweeping the streets, doorways, windows and rooftops around the building, leaned back into the car and said, "Okay, let's go. Quickly!" The three women walked quickly through the glass doors of the agency.

Linda Jordan stopped at the reception desk and glanced around at the comfortable surroundings.

"Margo," Katie said, "when you feel up to it, could you make Miss Jordan some hot tea? And perhaps a bite to eat?"

Margo nodded. "I'm better now that I'm on dry land."

Jane pulled in behind them, looking very flushed.

"I cannot believe that one of them insisted I must be Linda Jordan and tried to corner me for an interview."

"I hope you told him something very juicy," Linda Jordan offered. "I lead a rather dull life."

"Apparently you don't," Katie corrected her. "Janie, why don't you bring Linda into the conference room and get her settled? I need to talk to Alex for a minute."

Katie had read *The Franklin Cure* twice, unable to put it down each time. Like the millions of readers who had driven the novel to the best-seller list, breaking every known publishing record, she had been riveted by the nonstop thriller.

Linda Jordan broke not only literary ground, but all the rules of publishing by writing a fictional story about a young pre-med student, Kalen Michaels, who, while researching a paper on the history of cancer treatments, stumbles upon a formula for "eradicating ailments of a tumorous nature." The formula was written over two hundred years ago by a young man named Ebediah Franklin, nephew of Benjamin Franklin. In the book, Kalen Michaels convinces a progressive young doctor, and later love interest, to try the formula on a terminal patient. The results are dramatic. The action is nonstop as Kalen becomes targeted by assassins hired by a conglomerate of drug firms who fear the success of the Franklin Cure will bankrupt them overnight.

The novel became front-page news across the nation as desperate patients seeking one last hope attempted to replicate the formula, with mixed results. Some called *The Franklin Cure*, "a miracle waiting to happen," while others called it "an irresponsible atrocity playing off the emotions of the infirm and downtrodden," and decried Linda Jordan for toying with their loved ones in their greatest hour of need. Linda Jordan reluctantly appeared on several talk shows, imploring the public to use reason, reminding them that the book was fictional. However, she almost always followed up with the observation that she believed it was possible that the cure for cancer existed. She pointedly mentioned the billions of dollars that cancer research, treatments, and medicines generated, and stated that, were a cure to be brought forth, thousands of companies, hospitals, and medical research labs would, indeed, be bankrupted overnight.

The publishers of *The Franklin Cure* preempted lawsuits by printing a disclaimer, attached to each copy of the book. The disclaimer stated that no patient should disregard the advice of their medical professional. Unexplainably, several patients did show radical improvement after trying their own home version of *The Franklin Cure*, which was based on a combination of ancient herbs and tonics.

One year after its publication and uncharted success, the nonstop action movie version was now being filmed in Hollywood with an all-star cast, and *The Franklin Cure* was still flying off the shelves of bookstores. In the wake of its success, many "copycat" books had emerged.

Meanwhile, Linda Jordan was dubbed "that reclusive New Hampshire author" and "the next J. D. Salinger" because of her infrequent public appearances. Her publicist acknowledged that she preferred to live quietly in her newly acquired home, nestled "somewhere along the seacoast of New Hampshire." Sightings were rare, but when her face appeared on the cover of both *Newsweek* and *Time Magazine* as "one of the most controversial authors of our time," she was reluctantly thrust into the celebrity spotlight yet again and became instantly recognizable. Book sales continued to skyrocket.

Katie left Jane to tend to Linda Jordan while she slipped into their computer forensics lab, known as "The Cybercision Center." Alexandria Axelrod, her ex-hacker co-worker, sat hunched over a computer with her pet tarantula, Divinity, perched on her shoulder.

"Hey," Katie called.

Alexandria ignored her and focused instead on extracting a hard drive from a machine.

"So what's going on?"

"I'm pulling the hard drive on the Langevin case."

"I meant what's going on with your comment about our guest?"

"Nothing."

"Alex, it wasn't nothing. She almost got killed out on the water today."

Alexandria didn't flinch.

"She's in the conference room, and I'm going to go talk to her. Do you want to join me?"

"Not particularly, Katie."

"Can I ask why?"

"No."

"Alex…"

"It's personal."

KATIE STUDIED LINDA JORDAN for a few moments. Her short red hair was attractively cut in loose, curly layers, accentuating her almond-shaped green eyes. She had dark eyebrows that ran rather straight across her brows. She was neither beautiful nor unattractive, her face conveying intelligence more than anything else. Katie knew from her reading that she was in her early fifties, divorced, and was named one of the wealthiest bachelorettes in the Northeast. Katie watched Linda Jordan as she continued to nervously finger the silver fob around her neck.

"This is a lovely room," Linda said, glancing around at the staid surroundings, the mahogany-paneled walls and oversized chairs.

"Thank you. We are blessed with a business manager who also has quite a knack for interior decorating, even if she is a bit unsteady on the water."

Linda nodded. "What is this business exactly?" she asked.

"We never did get a chance to be properly introduced. I'm Katie Mahoney and this…," she said, gesturing widely, "is the Black Widow Investigative Agency, probably the safest place you can be right now."

Linda smiled. "Investigative Agency? You mean you're detectives?"

"Yes."

"Black widows?"

Katie laughed, always amused at the reaction the name of the agency evoked. "The bulk of our work involves getting the digital goods on husbands and boyfriends who have gone astray, hence the name."

"How clever," Linda said as Margo brought in a tray with tea and hot scones. Katie noted she seemed much steadier on her feet now.

"Can I get you anything else, Miss Jordan?" Margo asked as she poured the tea.

"No, thank you. This is fine. And the gentleman who rescued me? Is he a detective as well?"

Margo stifled a laugh while Katie answered.

"That gentleman is Antoine. His partner, Marcus, is Margo's twin brother. They own the interior design firm of Sachet & Sashay, located right next door."

"At some point, I'd like to thank him more formally."

"Of course."

"I'm very grateful to him and to the fact that you were all there."

"Believe it or not, you have a cheating husband to thank."

"I do?"

"We were on a surveillance assignment of another boat when all of this ...," she hesitated, "... activity happened."

"Yes, an unfortunate accident," Linda Jordan said as she sipped her tea.

"Miss Jordan ... Linda ... I believe the expression is 'taking literary license' to call what happened an accident. Particularly when it is highly rumored that you have received numerous death threats."

Linda set her teacup down very gently on the saucer. "I'm a reasonable woman, Katie. I'm trying to make sense of everything that has happened, the good and the bad, but the truth is, I don't know who to trust anymore. To be quite honest, I'm not even sure I'm safe here…"

Katie led Linda into the Cybercision Center.

Alexandria glanced over her shoulder, saw Linda Jordan, and turned back to her work.

"Don't mind my colleague," Katie said. "As you can see," she said gesturing at the stacks of computers awaiting a forensic examination, "we're a bit busy these days. Alexandria is an ex-hacker, now our technical security expert. She handles the bulk of the computer forensics work that we do."

"Computer forensics?" Linda asked.

"The in-depth examination of all files both currently present and formerly deleted, that reside on a computer's hard drive. Right now, Alex is looking at the contents of a hard drive that belongs to the gentleman piloting the other boat that we were doing surveillance on this morning."

"I see." Glancing at Divinity propped on Alexandria's shoulder, Linda leaned forward.

"Is that real?" she asked.

"Yes," Alexandria grunted, without making eye contact.

"How interesting."

"Alexandria knew you were here because as soon as we entered our parking lot, the movement triggered these cameras," Katie said, pointing to a bank of monitors mounted above them. "She could then zoom in," Katie said, as she zoomed in on her own car, "and capture the face of a visitor, utilizing facial recognition software to determine an identity. Barring that," she said, zooming in on her car's license plate that read, "BWA-1," "she could run the plate against the state's motor vehicle registrations to determine the owner. Every entry, every corner of this building is covered by security cameras that are automatically triggered by movement."

"Very impressive."

"In addition," Katie went on, "we employ a number of other internal security measures to ensure everyone's safety, though I'm sure you'll understand that I'd prefer not to elaborate." There was no need to explain the hidden cameras or the "truth chair" in the conference room that measured pulse and other vital signs as they were fed back to a computer-based program to determine if someone was telling the truth or not.

"Suffice it to say," Katie went on, "that we employ the latest technologies to ensure our safety and to make sure that every case we investigate is rock solid. An investigative agency's reputation is only as good as the number of successful cases it brings to fruition, and we have been most successful."

Linda Jordan nodded in appreciation.

"There's only one other tool we employ that stands above all of the technology you see here," she said gesturing around the room.

"And that is?"

"Women's intuition."

5

"I'VE BEEN WRITING ALL my life, but only professionally since my late thirties. A few of my other books did moderately well before I ever conceived of the idea for *The Franklin Cure*," Linda Jordan began. "I spent two years researching and writing it before I sent it off to my publisher, Ryan & Rogers. They are...were, I should say...a very small publishing house located in Maine. I liked the fact that they were small, nearby, and could give my manuscripts personal attention, unlike the huge publishing houses in New York City that pass a manuscript through as if it were on a conveyor belt in a factory, with a very short shelf life. Ryan & Rogers was committed to a solid marketing campaign."

"WE ALL HOPED THE book would do well, but neither I nor they had any clue that it would spark such controversy and be catapulted to the best-seller list. It is, after all, a work of fiction, fully contrived right here," she said, tapping her auburn hair. "It was never my intention to stir people's emotions to the point of having my life threatened. I suppose I should have taken the threats more seriously."

"Threats?" Katie asked.

"There have been many anonymous calls and letters. Many have been sent to my publisher, some to my agent, others to my publicist. I didn't take them very seriously until a few weeks ago. I recently purchased a new home that, like your offices, boasts a state-of-the-art security system connected to a twenty-four-hour security firm. I've kept the location of the house largely out of the press and it's fairly well hidden to ensure my privacy. About a month ago, I left to go to the marina to go out on my boat when I noticed a car following me."

"Did you get a plate? Any description?"

"It was a black sedan with a white man in the front seat."

"Did you see his face?"

"Only in profile."

"Was there anything distinctive about him?"

"He was big. Wide-necked. He had a dark cap on his head and wore glasses."

"Glasses? What kind? Aviator style, wire frame, plastic framed, frameless?"

"Tinted and sort of wraparound."

"What color?"

"Yellow."

"Wait a second," Katie said as she went quickly into her office. She pulled out a gear bag from a closet and rummaged through to find what she was looking for before returning to the conference room.

"Did they look like this?"

"Yes, that's exactly what they looked like," Linda said, examining the glasses with the tinted yellow safety lenses that wrapped around the frame.

"These are shooting glasses."

KATIE WATCHED THE COLOR drain from Linda's face. "You must be exhausted from this morning's ordeal. Would you like to lie down for a few minutes?"

"No … no thank you. I'll be alright."

"Can I offer you something stronger than tea?"

Linda nodded reticently. "Perhaps a spot of brandy, if you have it?"

Katie went to the mahogany cabinet, opened the doors, and took out a crystal decanter. She waited patiently as Linda sipped the Courvoisier and noted the color coming back to her face. Linda set the snifter down on the table beside her.

"Better?"

"Much. Thank you. Anyway, the car followed me all the way to the marina. I was so afraid by that point that I called the police, but the car sped off before they got there. Two weeks later, I attended a well-publicized book signing where another incident occurred."

Katie nodded, having read about it in all the local papers.

"The Laketon Police Department was notified of my appearance prior to the event. I met with one of the captains who took care of posting a police officer outside the doors as a precaution."

"Do you remember this captain's name?"

"Hmmm… It will come to me. He was quite tall and good looking, in a Tom Selleck kind of way, with a very nice moustache and thick eyebrows."

Katie bit her lip. "Joe Kennedy?"

"Yes!" Linda said gesturing toward Katie. "That was his name. He was very kind and sweet, and seemed genuinely concerned. Do you know him?"

CAPTAIN JOE KENNEDY WAS indeed tall, with dark, wavy hair, green eyes, and a thick moustache that gave him a striking resemblance to Tom Selleck. Katie had been on the job at the Laketon Police Department for two years when they found themselves physically drawn to each other. Because Joe was her supervisor, they had to be extra discreet about their relationship, which made everything that much more exciting. They were married a year later. Policy mandated that they not work directly together, so Katie transferred to the Narcotics Division while Joe remained in Patrol.

It was during the worst time of their marriage, a time when Katie was equally as immersed in undercover work as in a bottle of scotch, that Joe, who felt largely ignored, fell for the attentions of a young police reporter, Chelsea Mattox. Chelsea's dark, wild hair and nearly black eyes were a stark contrast to Katie's fair Celtic coloring and light blue eyes. Whereas Katie was always fighting off extra pounds, Chelsea had a near-perfect body with pencil-thin legs, high, perky breasts, and a small ass. She dressed, always, to show off her assets.

The affair was short-lived, but as soon as Katie found out about it, her cover was blown during an undercover narcotics operation.

The bullet that tore through her uterus when the deal went bad left her infertile. It wasn't until much later that Katie learned that Chelsea Mattox might have been the one responsible for blowing her cover. Chelsea had been working on an expose about a young, up-and-coming drug lord around the same time Katie was negotiating a drug deal with the same young man. Joe, when pressed for a reason why his wife was never around, accidentally divulged Katie's undercover work. Chelsea feigned innocence, claiming not to realize that Katie was in fact, an undercover detective. Katie found Chelsea Mattox's story hard to believe, considering the fact that her picture sat on the corner of Joe's desk.

"THOUSANDS OF PEOPLE TURNED out to the book signing," Linda said, "so it ran much later than anticipated. A young police officer posted outside the door insisted on escorting me to my car afterward. I thanked him, got in my car and left. A few minutes later, I noticed the same dark-colored sedan following me. It was late and there wasn't that much traffic. I deliberately made several abrupt turns and he stayed behind me the whole way. At one point, the car sped up and attempted to come along beside me. I tried to get a license plate number, which is what Captain Kennedy had advised me to do, but it was too dark and the license plate lights were out."

"What did you do?"

"I turned around and drove straight back to the Laketon Police Department. Captain Kennedy was on duty. He came out and followed me home. The other car was gone. Captain Kennedy stayed with me for some time and said he would make sure there would be extra patrols."

"Did you tell anyone else about it?"

"I mentioned it to Carly Ryan, my publisher. She was quite concerned."

Katie mulled this over and studied Linda as she raised her hand to her mouth to try and stifle a huge yawn. Her hand dropped to her chest and she rubbed the silver fob yet again.

"Forgive me," Linda said. "I suddenly feel very tired."

"Understandable, but if you don't mind, I have just a few more questions, in particular about that silver ..."

"Yoo-hoo!" Katie heard as the door was suddenly flung open and Marcus entered, carrying a copy of *The Franklin Cure*, followed reluctantly by Antoine, followed by Margo, who gave Katie a big shrug, followed by Jane, who peered over Margo's shoulder.

"Sorry, Katarina darling, but we've never had anyone quite so famous in our little parlor and I just had to see if the Divine Miss Jordan would be so kind ..."

Linda Jordan made an effort to smile. "Of course. In fact I was hoping to be formally introduced to my hero so that I might properly thank him," she said as she rose and gave Antoine a handshake that awkwardly became a hug with several pats on the back.

"This seaman is spoken for, dear," Marcus said, stepping in between them and squeezing Antoine's arm. Margo swatted her brother on the arm.

"Don't start, Marcus," she said. "We have a guest."

"Then you're very lucky to have someone so brave in your life," Linda said.

Katie clapped her hands at the group. "Excuse me, people, but we were in the middle of something ..."

"Miss Jordan, could I, your hero's life partner, ask you to autograph this copy? Perhaps, 'To my dear friend, Marcus, designer extraordinaire,' would work."

Linda politely obliged.

"You can just say, 'To Margo' on mine."

"Oh dear, I left my copy at home," Jane said, with much disappointment.

Katie snapped her fingers. "Alright, that's enough. You all have work to do, don't you?"

"My, my, someone's a bit testy today," Marcus threw over his shoulder as they shuffled back out.

"Forgive the interruption, Linda."

"Not to worry. I always appreciate my readers' enthusiasm."

"As I was about to say …," Katie began as she eyed the silver fob, but Linda quickly interrupted.

"If you don't mind," she said. "I am rather exhausted and still damp with saltwater. What I'd really love is to find a place to shower …"

"You've come to the right place then," Katie said with a slight note of disappointment for having to wait again. "Let me show you to our facilities."

Katie led Linda to their ladies room, complete with the large shower surrounded in Moroccan tile.

"This is lovely!" Linda noted. "And quite unexpected."

"We like to go first class all the way."

"So I see. But I don't have any clean clothes."

"Not a problem. You and Jane appear to be about the same size if you don't mind elastic waists."

Linda rested her hand on Katie's arm for a second and smiled weakly.

"Right now, elastic waists sound splendid."

IT WAS SOME TIME before Linda reemerged, looking much restored. Katie noted that the chain with the silver fob had a bit of soap caught in it. Jane's flowered poly-cotton blend top with the bright hibiscus flowers and polyester stretch pants did little to emphasize Linda Jordan's trim figure, but she still looked more comfortable.

"Fashionista, Jane's not," Katie said apologetically, but Linda shook her head.

"It's better than damp and salty, trust me."

They returned to the conference room.

"I have a few more questions if you don't mind," Katie said, eyeing the silver fob. "In particular, I'd like to ask you about that silver ..." The door was abruptly flung open as Alexandria stuck her head in. Alexandria ignored Linda Jordan completely.

"I need to talk to you for a minute, Katie."

ALEXANDRIA SWUNG THE MONITOR around so Katie could see it. Katie looked at the view from the outside cameras that pointed down the street and noticed a black sedan moving away from the camera.

"This same car has been circling around the area ever since you arrived with Miss Cure All."

"Can you get a plate?"

"Yes, but it's not on file with the State DMV. Possible phony plate or tape on it to change the digits."

"What about the driver? Any luck there?"

Alex rewound the video until the car was parallel to the camera's angle. She zoomed in on the driver's face that was largely obscured by a baseball cap and dark sunglasses.

"Do you think it's something?" Alex asked.

"Oh yeah," Katie said studying the monitor. "It's something alright."

"What do you want to do?"

Katie paced back and forth. "If she's in danger, we're all in danger. How in the world could they have found her ..." Katie paused and winced when she remembered the only other person to know Linda Jordan's whereabouts. She shook her head. "I'll deal with that later. For now, we're going to have to take care of this problem."

"Good luck," Alexandria said in a dismissive tone.

"Alex, whatever your issue is with her, I need you to put your personal feelings aside, be professional, and get the job done. Understood?"

Alexandria took Divinity off her shoulder and very carefully set her into her glass aquarium.

"Sure, Katie, whatever you say," Alexandria said, flashing her nearly black eyes.

"WE HAVE A SLIGHT problem," Katie said as they all assembled in the Black Widow Agency conference room. "That same black sedan that has been giving you trouble appears to be in the area."

"But how did they ... I thought ...," Linda began to say as she turned to Jane.

"I'm sure I wasn't followed, Katie," Jane said vehemently. "I watched everyone around me and drove around three times."

"It wasn't you, Janie. It was a certain reporter who is the bane of my existence these days. In any case, we need to act quickly."

Linda instinctively reached for the silver fob.

"Katie," Alexandria said as she brought up the big screen in the conference room displaying the outside cameras. They all watched as the black sedan slowed down and pulled across the street from their building.

"Let me know if he moves," Katie said as she quickly slipped out of the room and into her office. Unlike the rest of the Black Widow Agency that was adorned with a mixture of mahoganies and soft, nature-inspired décor, Katie's office looked like it had been transported from her old police station. The desk was solid maple and well-gouged. Her trusty forty millimeter was in the top drawer and her fifth of Glenlivet in the bottom. The desktop was cluttered with an assortment of case-related papers and magazines germane to computer forensics. Hanging on the wall opposite her desk was her beloved shirtless Tom Selleck poster. Katie unlocked the top drawer and grabbed her forty-millimeter Sig, checked that the magazine was fully loaded and the safety on, put an extra magazine into her pocket, and clipped the holster and a pair of handcuffs onto her belt. She slipped a navy-blue blazer on over that.

"HE'S STILL SITTING THERE," Alexandria informed her when she returned.

"Fine. If he wants to tangle with the Black Widows, then welcome to our Home Sweet Web. Now here's the plan…"

TEN MINUTES LATER, JANE, once again wearing the blue straw hat and a pair of sunglasses, walked out of the offices of the Black Widow Agency and headed toward Linda Jordan's green Jaguar that Marcus had driven over from the Coast Guard Station. She slid in and glanced in the rearview mirror.

"Don't hurt your back," she said to Katie, who was already crouched down in the back seat.

"Don't worry about me," Katie said. "Just do exactly what I told you."

Jane waited until Margo and Alexandria got in their cars before pulling out of the back parking lot and onto the street. Jane noted the sedan pull in behind them. The others were well behind the black sedan as she made the turns that Katie had instructed her to until they neared Boyea Alley.

"We're near the alley," Jane announced.

"Good. Just do what I told you."

"I'm nervous, Katie. I think I feel a hot flash coming on."

Katie, who was miserably uncomfortable jammed down in the back seat, rolled her eyes. "You're doing fine, Janie," she said reassuringly. "Just do like I said. Think of little MaryJane."

"Did I mention she's pulling herself up?"

Katie tried to not think of the cramp in her back.

Jane drove slowly down the street, checking to make sure the black sedan was behind them, then, as instructed, abruptly sped up and turned right into the alley. The black sedan sped up to catch her and without realizing they were going into a dead end, pulled in behind her. Realizing he was trapped, the driver quickly threw the car in reverse, but Margo and Alexandria pulled in behind him and blocked his escape. Katie sprang into action, leaping out of the car as she drew her weapon and faced the startled driver.

"Get your hands on the wheel!" Katie screamed, gun drawn and finger alongside the trigger. The man's mouth parted slightly as he put both his hands on the steering column. Katie opened the driver's door and ordered him out and to lean on the hood. Recalling her years of training as a police officer, she spread the man's legs apart to throw his balance off and quickly patted him down. She felt the bulge under his left arm, pulled open his shirt and withdrew a nine-millimeter Smith & Wesson semi-automatic from a shoulder holster, which she quickly tucked into her own waistband. She handcuffed him behind his back and spun him around.

"Please!" he said. "It's not what you think."

Katie whipped his baseball cap and sunglasses off. The man was in his mid-thirties with a "high and tight" military-style haircut, buzzed on the sides with just a small tuft of dark hair on top. He was wearing a tank shirt with a blue overshirt and blue jeans. He was much taller than Katie, with a muscular build and a very wide neck. He could easily have fought with her and likely won, gun or no gun.

"Who are you?" Katie demanded.

"Who am I? Who the hell are you?"

Katie waved the gun in his face. "I'm the one with the gun, so I'm the one who gets to ask the questions. Now who are you?"

The man looked at the assorted lot of women grimacing at him, one older woman, obviously not Linda Jordan, who kept fanning herself and sweating profusely; one young, tall, and thin, dark-haired woman with pale skin and near-black eyes; and one large black woman holding an umbrella menacingly and snapping it in her palms repeatedly.

"He gives you one bad move and I'll whip his ass," Margo announced as she shook the umbrella at the man.

"I'm losing my patience," Katie said, "Who are you?"

"I'm supposed to be …," he said as his head went from side to side.

"Supposed to be what?" Katie asked twisting the weight of the gun in her hand.

Realizing he had no choice, the man reluctantly said, "My ID is in my back right pocket."

Katie carefully withdrew the slim leather case from his jeans and flipped it open. She relaxed her stance and reholstered her weapon, but kept the man handcuffed.

"Let's go," she said as she directed him back to the car. "You have some explaining to do."

LINDA JORDAN WAS SAFELY hidden away in Marcus and Antoine's design firm, Sachet & Sashay, but returned as Katie led the handcuffed man into the conference room. Katie deliberately seated him in the chair that would monitor his vital signs to determine if he was telling the truth. She then gestured to Alexandria to monitor his responses. Alexandria retrieved a laptop and discreetly set it on her lap.

"Talk," Katie commanded.

"Could you take these off?" he asked.

"I'll take them off when I'm satisfied with your answers."

The man looked anxiously at the women, but focused his attention on Linda Jordan.

"I'm not here to harm her," he began. "My name is Steve Donahue. I'm with Seamus Security."

KATIE KNEW THE FIRM well. Seamus Security was started up by a former colleague of hers, Eddie Seamus, an ex-Laketon cop of dubious integrity. Though Katie never denied that in her worst days leading up to her divorce and the shooting, she occasionally showed up for work still feeling the influence from a prior drink, Eddie made it a habit of keeping a bottle of Jameson in his locker and his cruiser. If Eddie's house needed painting, he suddenly managed to arrest a bunch of painters until one of them was willing to deal. He never paid for food anywhere in the confines of Laketon and was finally fired after getting caught setting up pinhole cameras in the women's shower at the department. He started up his own private security firm touting his police credentials, much to Katie's dismay. Eddie's reputation for drinking on the job and hiring mindless thugs, ex-crooks, and dirty cops who were on the take far outweighed his reputation for hiring skilled employees.

"Seamus Security?" Linda said rather surprised. "But I only hired you people to install an alarm system in my house."

"I'm not working for you right now, Miss Jordan," Steve Donahue replied.

"Then who are you working for?"

"That I can't say."

Katie stared at him. "You don't have much of a choice, Mr. Donahue."

Margo snapped the umbrella loudly and sneered at him.

"Fine," he said nervously as he glanced at her. "I was hired by her publishers, Ryan & Rogers."

"What?" Linda said. "They would never …"

"They would and they did."

Linda dropped into a chair. "I can't believe this."

"Where were you at ten thirty this morning?" Katie asked.

"Waiting for Miss Jordan to get back from her boat trip."

"Can you prove it?"

Donahue, who was handcuffed in the front, abruptly reached into his jacket pocket, which prompted Katie to place her hand on her holstered gun. The man saw her and slowly withdrew a bright orange ticket. He leaned forward and passed it to Katie.

"I got ticketed for sitting in the marina parking lot without a permit."

Katie glanced first at the ticket, then at Alexandria to confirm the man was telling the truth. When Alexandria nodded ever-so-slightly, Katie got up and uncuffed him.

"Who told you she was here?"

Steve Donahue rubbed both of his wrists with his hands. "There's a girl I know. We dated a few times. She was at the Coast Guard Station."

"Does this girl happen to be a reporter?"

"Yes."

"So let me get this straight. Linda's publishers hired you to protect her...from what?"

"I wasn't hired to protect her," he said.

"I don't understand."

"I was hired to protect that," he said as he pointed to the silver fob wrapped around Linda Jordan's neck.

KATIE SENT STEVE DONAHUE on his way with instructions that he was officially "off-duty." She then sent the others back to their offices so she could speak to Linda alone.

Linda held the silver fob in her hand as Katie poured them both another glass of brandy.

"May I see that?" Katie finally asked as she handed Linda her glass.

Linda set the glass down, slipped the chain off of her neck and handed the silver fob over to Katie. Katie saw a seam line and tried to open the fob up, but it wouldn't budge.

"Here," Linda said pointing to where the fob connected to the chain, "that's the release button."

Katie pressed on the connector and the fob slipped apart. Katie looked at its contents and shook her head.

"It's a thumb drive," Katie observed.

Linda held out her hand, reconnected it, and quickly slipped it back around her neck. "And if all goes well, this little thumb drive will be worth about forty million dollars in one week's time."

"Forty million dollars?" Katie asked, nearly spilling her drink.

"It's the sequel to *The Franklin Cure*. It's the only copy that exists. I have one more week's worth of editing before I have to submit it to my publisher."

"Isn't it dangerous to have just one copy? Suppose you had lost it in the ocean this morning. Suppose it got wet?"

"It's completely waterproof. As for the one copy, if I'm going to go down, I'd prefer to take it with me. I know that sounds odd, but with what this manuscript is worth, I can't risk someone accidentally getting access to it. If they got hold of it, it would be leaked across the Internet in a matter of days and be worth nothing. So you see, Katie, it's imperative that I keep it safe. It's worth forty million to me if it gets delivered, two million to someone else if it does not."

"I don't understand."

"There's a two-million-dollar bounty for it," Linda said touching the fob. "I told you the book upset a lot of people. I can't tell you much about the sequel except to say it is equally controversial, and will stir the proverbial pot again. There are many people, pharmaceutical manufacturers, disgruntled patients, and families of patients who would prefer I just dropped off the face of the earth, or, fell into the ocean like this morning. The word is that someone is willing to pay two million dollars to make sure the sequel does not get published. That's why I've been trying to stay low key and out of sight so I could just finish it and get it to Ryan & Rogers. The only problem is that I'm scheduled to appear at a publicity event Wednesday evening for the Laketon Public Library. They've just completed the addition of an outdoor reading room and park which I partially funded and I am supposed to help with the ribbon cutting."

"Can't you cancel?"

"Not really. I committed to do it months ago and the library has blown its entire publicity budget advertising my appearance to help raise the rest of the money for the project. I really don't want to let them down."

"Let me think about that. In the meantime, who knew you would be out on your boat this morning?"

"No one."

"You live alone?"

"Yes."

"You didn't tell anyone? Mention it on the phone perhaps, to a friend? Lover?"

Linda smiled. "I've been a bit too busy and reclusive for either lately."

"Are you sure you didn't mention it to anyone?"

Linda looked pensively at the fabric on the chair.

"Come to think of it, I did mention it in an e-mail to Carly Ryan, the co-publisher at Ryan & Rogers, but I know Carly wants this book to be published more than anyone. I mean, after all, their continued fortune depends on this getting published."

"Did you send this e-mail from your own computer?"

"Yes."

"The laptop that went overboard?"

"No, my home computer."

"I'm going to need to look at that computer."

"May I ask why?"

"It's very possible someone has tapped into it and is monitoring your e-mail. I have to tell you that if that's the case, it's also possible that your computer could have malware, such as a keystroke logger, planted on it and that your keystrokes may have been recorded."

"I'm not worried about that," Linda said satisfactorily.

"Why not?"

"I never use a computer connected to the Internet to type my books. I always work on laptops that have no Internet connection. In fact, I never save anything on the laptop, just on this portable drive. Mr. Seamus had one of his people come over and he suggested that."

"Really?"

Katie found it quite interesting that Eddie Seamus thought he was qualified to give digital security advice.

"ARE ANY OF THE laptops that you write on connected to a printer?"

"Yes. I have a printer that is shared with my computers and my laptops wirelessly. Is ... is that a problem?"

Katie shook her head. "There's such a thing as tunneling through the network to gain access to other devices. It's also very possible to retrieve print jobs."

"Oh dear. They never mentioned that."

Katie resisted the temptation to say, "I'm not surprised." Instead, she bit her tongue and said, "It's not well known, unless you have a lot of expertise in the area."

Linda pondered this. "It seems to me that your firm has provided a great deal more services in one day than Seamus Security has in the last few months. I wonder ..."

"Yes?"

"Would your agency be available to see that this," she said fingering the fob "... gets delivered safely?"

"I think that could be arranged."

"And since you know so much about computers, perhaps you could help me with making sure my work is secure?"

"Absolutely."

"Then other than getting me through Wednesday night and the library appearance ..."

"There's just one more thing," Katie said interrupting. "A reporter I'm familiar with has asked for an exclusive interview with you within the week."

"I'm afraid that's out of the question until the sequel is completed."

"I understand."

"Is this a personal friend?"

Katie laughed. "Hardly. More of a nemesis who can wreak havoc with my life and the agency's reputation if she doesn't get her way."

"I see," Linda said, mulling this over. "Perhaps if I can just find somewhere safe to stay and finish the editing, I might be available. It would be good to make the announcement that the book is out of my hands. I just need to find a quiet place to work out of the public eye."

"I have an idea about that," Katie said lifting her brandy glass. "By any chance, do you like Jack Daniels?"

Linda Jordan tilted her head at the question. "I've been known to have a glass or two."

"I may know just the place…"

KATIE MAHONEY WALKED INTO the Shamrock Shores Assisted Living Facility, which she affectionately called "Little Ireland," carrying a wooden liquor crate in her arms. Shamrock Shores was reputed to be a "dry" facility because the residents weren't supposed to mix alcohol with the myriad of medications they were taking, but Katie, along with everyone else, knew better. The liquor box immediately caught the eye of the Shamrock Shores Director, Gracelyn MacDougal, who glanced up from behind her desk.

Gracelyn MacDougal had dull, brown hair and overly large brown eyes that gave her the appearance of always staring, a feature Katie attributed to either the misfortune of bad genes or an overactive thyroid. Gracelyn dressed like the senior residents who were twenty or more years older than she. She wore a paisley print dress buttoned all the way up and a cardigan sweater draped over her shoulders with the top button fastened. She rarely used makeup and always wore sturdy, orthopedic shoes. There was no question, however, that she ran the Shamrock Shores facility with efficiency. Though Katie was not her biggest fan, she had to admire the fact that the woman spent the bulk of her day with old people and seemed to enjoy it.

Katie walked right past Gracelyn MacDougal's office and peeked into "The Emerald Room," where she spotted her mother knitting and chatting with two other residents, Mrs. Timmons and Mrs. McAfee. Molly Mahoney raised her knitting needles in recognition of her daughter and gestured with her head for Katie to come over. Katie leaned over to give her mother a small kiss on the cheek just as Gracelyn MacDougal arrived at her side.

"Hello, Ms. Mahoney," Gracelyn said, eyeing the liquor crate. Katie had no choice but to turn and acknowledge her presence.

"Hello, Mrs. MacDougal," Katie said as pleasantly as she could, feigning a smile for her mother's sake.

Gracelyn MacDougal was several inches shorter than Katie and tried, as unobtrusively as she could, to see what was inside the liquor box. Katie knew Gracelyn MacDougal was not going to go anywhere until she was satisfied that there was no booze in the box. Reluctantly, she set it down on the floor right in front of her and took out a large plastic bag that was nestled inside the box and handed it to her mother. Gracelyn MacDougal, seeing that the box was now empty, relaxed her stance.

"Here's all the family pictures I could find, Ma," Katie announced.

Her mother carefully set her knitting needles in her lap, glanced down at the empty box with a perplexed look on her face, and took the bag from her daughter. Gracelyn MacDougal stood over them like a hawk circling around its prey.

"She's making a scrapbook," Katie announced to all. Gracelyn MacDougal watched as Molly Mahoney dug through the bag and pulled out a picture.

"Oh look," Molly said pulling out a picture and showing it to Mrs. Timmons and Mrs. McAfee. "This was Katie wearing her father's uniform hat when she was five years old. And here's a picture of the two of them standing together in uniform when she graduated from the police academy." She passed the photo around.

Mrs. McAfee looked at it, smiled, and said, "I have almost the same photo with my Boyd and his father. Did you ever meet my Boyd, Katie?"

Katie shook her head. "The name doesn't sound familiar. What Division was he in?"

"Fourteenth."

Katie shook her head again. "I was in the Third my entire career."

"He's single, you know. Divorced, actually."

Katie smiled politely. "I'll keep it in mind, Mrs. McAfee, but I really don't have much free time these days."

Molly Mahoney waited for Gracelyn MacDougal to retreat back to her office before confronting her daughter. She looked at the empty box and said very quietly, "I thought you were going... shopping... for me, dear." Katie looked at her mother, then nodded cautiously toward the two other women beside her.

"Can these two be trusted?" Katie asked.

Molly Mahoney looked at her friends, whose curiosity was now aroused.

"These two? Why Katie, I'd trust these two with my life."

"You may have to. Check this out," Katie said as she reached down and slid the empty liquor box closer to all of them. Glancing around to make sure no one else was looking, Katie pushed down on one corner of the bottom of the box. It immediately flipped up. She grabbed the corner of the bottom and pulled it out. Nestled in the bottom and wrapped in see-through bubble wrap to prevent breakage and clanking, were two bottles of Jack Daniels.

"Sweet, Mary, there is a Lord," said Mrs. Timmons.

"Amen to that," said Mrs. McAfee.

"Aye, she's a good girl, my Katie," Molly Mahoney announced proudly, "and a clever one. Imagine that, making something look perfectly normal when in fact, it's full of secrets."

"Clever perhaps," Katie explained, "but certainly not original. The drug dealers used false bottoms all the time to hide their drugs. Just an old trick I learned on the job."

Molly Mahoney looked over her shoulder and said, "In any case, ladies, the card game is in my room tonight."

"Katie, dear," said Mrs. Timmons, "I don't suppose if I gave you some money that you could perhaps…"

"Oh now Annie, you can't ask her to start running booze for you," Molly said.

Mrs. Timmons looked genuinely disappointed. "But I asked my girl and she said that's why they put me in here in the first place. Can you imagine?"

"Don't you worry, Annie," Molly said patting her friend's arm, "there's more than enough to go around and I'm sure if I ask Katie, she can restock us whenever we need it."

Katie laughed. "Sure, Ma, I'll sneak men into your room too, if you'd like."

"Oh, she doesn't need to, not with Timothy Collins around," said Mrs. McAfee. Mrs. Timmons stifled a giggle.

"Oh?" Katie said with raised eyebrows.

"Oh for the Good Lord's sakes, Peggy," Molly Mahoney began. "Now don't you go putting crazy ideas in her head. Without his hearing aids, he's as deaf as a tree," her mother explained defensively. "I have to get close to him to get him to understand anything I say. Besides, he can't hear me with the likes of you two yakking all the time."

"Well then he must be blind as well, because he seems to have to stare at you a lot, too," Mrs. McAfee said. The two women laughed.

"Ach," Molly Mahoney said waving her hand, "don't listen to these two old birds, Katie. They're senile."

"Senile, huh?" Katie said. "Sounds to me like their faculties are sharp as can be."

"If their faculties get any sharper," Molly Mahoney said firmly, "they can forget about the card game in my room later on." She tapped the box with her toe for emphasis. The two women immediately stifled their smiles, retrieved their knitting needles, and got back to work.

"Ma, could I maybe talk to you for a few minutes in your room before Mrs. MacDragon comes back?"

Mrs. McAfee and Mrs. Timmons laughed out loud. "You see, Molly, we're not the only ones who call her that!"

Molly Mahoney shook her head, "Senile and rude," Molly said as she gathered up her needles. She tapped the box with her foot.

"Just make sure this comes with us. I don't trust these two for one second now that they know what's in it."

"I thought you trusted us with your life," Peggy McAfee said feigning hurt feelings.

"I do trust you with my life," Molly Mahoney said as she rose from her chair. Glancing around and lowering her voice, she added, "It's my booze I wouldn't leave either one of you alone with."

ONCE INSIDE HER MOTHER's apartment, Katie removed the bottles from the false bottom and unwrapped them.

"Where do you want them?"

"Oh, they go in my underwear drawer in the bedroom. Second drawer down in the dresser."

"You keep your booze in your underwear drawer?"

"Katie," her mother began, "if this place should ever go up in flames, the Good Lord preventing," she added for good measure, "there are three things I want to take with me. Clean underwear, your father's badge, and something to calm my nerves. All three I keep together just in case."

Katie laughed and went into her mother's bedroom. She gently tucked the bottles in the drawer alongside another half-empty bottle of Jack Daniels. She saw her father's leather badge case and sat down on the edge of the bed with it. The silver was tarnished and she made a mental note to bring some silver polish over the next time. She touched the edges of it, felt the heaviness of the metal and remembered the day her father had pinned her badge on her own uniform, a tradition in the Laketon Police Department when another family member was on the force. Although she had plenty of phony badges tucked away in her old wooden desk in her office, Katie's original badge had been stripped from her the day she was terminated for tampering with evidence in Margo's case, but Katie knew in her heart that the young mother had been set up by her husband who had asked her to deliver a knapsack. Margo had no clue that it was filled with cocaine until she handed it over to Katie, who promptly arrested her. But as Katie interrogated Margo, her instincts told her Margo was an innocent victim, even if no one else believed her. Katie put her career on the line when she stole into the evidence room and removed the cocaine, unaware that she was on videotape the whole time.

KATIE RUBBED HER LATE father's badge gently with the sleeve of her blouse. She turned to see her mother standing in the doorway watching her.

"That will be yours someday, Katie," her mother said, "but for now it's the last piece I have of him."

Katie felt herself uncharacteristically choking up and cleared her throat. "I'll bring some silver polish over next time," she said. "It's getting a bit tarnished."

"Don't bother," her mother said. "When it's yours you can polish it all you want. For now, I'd like to think we're aging together."

Katie pulled herself together, cleared her throat again, and walked back out into the kitchen. Her mother set a cup of tea down in front of her.

Katie studied her mother for a second. Although she had aged quite a bit since Katie's father had died and at times could move like an old woman, Molly Mahoney still had a youthful grace about her. She wore her thick, curly long gray hair tucked up, always in a bun. She and Katie shared the same light blue-gray eyes.

"Have you seen your sister lately, Katie?"

Molly Mahoney was well-aware of the tension that often came between her daughter, the ex-cop, and her other daughter, Kelly, the public defender.

"In fact, I bumped into her in court the other day. She's worried about your relationship with Timothy Collins."

Katie watched her mother's expression change. "Oh for heaven's sakes, I don't have any 'relationship' with Timothy Collins. We're good friends. That's all. Why on earth would your sister be concerned about that?"

"You know, Kelly, Ma. She just wants to make sure that Timothy Collins isn't going to have his way with you and then steal your life savings."

Katie watched the color rise on her mother's cheeks. "Katie, if you were any younger, I'd wash your mouth out with soap for such inappropriate talk."

"It was Kelly who said it, Ma, not me. I'm just reiterating what she said."

"Regardless, Timothy Collins is a friend. We're all friends here. You know, Katie," her mother began as she dipped her tea bag in and out of her cup, "I will tell you that I was not thrilled to have to come here in the beginning."

"I remember, Ma."

"As much as I miss the old house, I've come to find it very convenient to not have to worry about its upkeep. In some ways, it has given me a great deal of freedom and I enjoy spending that time with the many wonderful people here. Of course, there's always a slightly damaged apple in the bunch here and there, but for the most part, everyone gets along and I do enjoy my new friends, including Mr. Timothy Collins. Now as for him having his way with me, honestly Katie..."

Katie laughed and reached over to touch her mother's cheek. "Ma, you know you're still a knockout."

"The only thing that is knocked out these days," her mother began, "is my old body. Knocked out of whack, I might add."

"So tell me about Timothy Collins," Katie said.

"I told you, Katie. He was a state trooper. He retired from the criminal investigations division and he and your father met a few times over cases. He's pleasant and companionable and we enjoy reminiscing. He really is deaf as a doornail unless he's wearing his hearing aids, and half the time he forgets to. He's been widowed for ten years now. He absolutely adored his wife, Betsy. In fact, he's told me a few times that I remind him of her, so you see, Katie, that's all it is. When you lose someone and then find someone that reminds you of them in a certain way, you want to get close to that person because it keeps you close to the memory." Molly sipped her tea. "Now what was it you wanted to be talking to me about?"

"I have a big favor to ask."

"Oh?"

"I need to hide someone for a few days."

"Who?"

"Someone very famous."

Molly's eyes perked up. Katie knew that although Molly denied knowing anything about "those sinful Hollywood types" that every night, she and many of the other residents were glued to the television at seven p.m., watching *Entertainment Tonight*. Though they decried everything about the loss of morality, no episode was ever missed and the single copy of *People Magazine* that arrived weekly at Shamrock Shores was well-worn by the time it made its rounds.

"Who is it, Katie?"

Katie leaned forward and whispered the name into her mother's ear.

"You've met her? I just saw the previews for the movie. It's going to star Betty Barron and Evan Duke. Of course, Betty Barron is divorcing her second husband and the rumor is that she and Evan …"

"Ma, I need to know if she could stay here."

"Stay here?" Molly asked. "You mean here at Shamrock Shores?"

"Actually, I need her to stay right here in your room. You have the empty spare room. It would just be for a few days and she'll be busy editing her book the whole time. You won't even know she's here. It's the only safe place I can think of …"

"Safe? Is she in danger?"

"Possibly, but if she stays here in your room, no one will ever know where she is. I won't let anything happen to either one of you, Ma, I promise."

"Imagine someone that famous right here at Shamrock Shores. Annie and Peggy won't believe it."

"Ma, you've got to promise me you won't tell anyone. Seriously, she's only safe if you don't tell anyone."

"But we were supposed to have our card game here tonight …"

"And that works out perfectly. I'll bring her in as soon as you're done."

"But they lock the doors at night."

"I'll deal with that."

"Katie," her mother admonished, "I don't like the idea of you breaking in. It isn't right."

"I'd ask you to unlock the door, but I don't want to risk having you traipsing around and drawing attention." She saw her mother's hesitation. "You don't have to do this, Ma. I can bring her to my apartment, but ..."

"But you and Joe ..."

"We have been seeing a lot of each other lately."

"I'm happy for you," Molly said touching her daughter's hand. "I always liked Joe, you know that. He's a good man."

"We had ... have ... a lot of things to work through."

"Good for you, Katie."

"It really wouldn't be a problem though, if you'd prefer not to ..."

"Don't be silly, Katie. In fact, it might be nice to have a little company here if she doesn't mind staying with a boring old lady."

"I doubt she'll find you the least bit boring, Ma."

Molly realized something and frowned. "There's just one thing, Katie."

"What's that?"

"Does she like Jack Daniels?"

KATIE WAITED OUTSIDE IN the white Black Widow Agency van with "Divinity Florals" on the side until her mother called.

"The girls are just getting ready to leave now," her mother whispered from her bedroom phone. Katie could hear laughter and the clinking of glasses in the background.

Turning around to Linda Jordan, Katie said, "It's time."

Linda clutched a large shopping bag that contained her laptop and some clothes and straightened out the gray wig perched on her head. She tugged down at the oversized, shapeless floral dress she was wearing. Katie closed the door to the van very quietly as she led Linda to the front doors of Shamrock Shores. Reaching into her pocket, she took out a small leather pouch and pulled out a thin rod that had teeth on the end of it. Katie quickly slipped it into the door and jiggled it back and forth until she heard a small "click." She turned the doorknob and looked in.

The sound of a television came blaring from the Emerald Room. Katie glanced anxiously toward Gracelyn MacDougal's office, but was relieved to see the lights were out. She motioned for Linda Jordan to stay behind her as they walked slowly down the halls. As they approached the Emerald Room, Katie leaned across the door frame and saw Timothy Collins, with his thick head of full white hair, watching the Jay Leno Show. Katie tucked her arm under Linda's arm as if escorting her and walked normally past the doorway.

"Molly, is that you?" she heard Timothy call just as they passed by.

Katie gestured for Linda to keep going but realized that Timothy was rising, albeit slowly, from his chair and heading toward them.

"It's me, Mr. Collins," she said stepping into the doorway, cutting off his path. "Molly's daughter, Katie Mahoney."

"Who's full of baloney?" Timothy shouted.

Katie glanced anxiously toward Gracelyn's office, knowing her small utilitarian apartment sat right behind it.

"Good night, Mr. Collins," Katie said, smiling.

"What's not right? Where's Molly?"

"She's going to bed," Katie said. "To bed," she said again, louder.

"Good night, then," he said as he settled himself back down into the chair.

"MA, MEET LINDA JORDAN. Linda, this is my mother, Molly Mahoney."

"Thank you so much for your offer to put me up," Linda said offering her hand.

Molly stumbled slightly as she leaned forward to shake Linda's hand. Katie looked over to see the empty Jack Daniels bottles on the counter.

"The pleasure and honor are mine," Molly said with somewhat slurred speech. Molly held onto Linda's hand and did not let it go. Katie began to rethink the whole idea. If Linda noticed her mother's condition, she said nothing.

"Let me show you to your room," Molly said, but as she stepped forward, she stumbled again. Katie reached for her.

"Ma, why don't you go to bed and I'll help Linda get settled in, okay?

Her mother turned to her. "I think I'm old enough to tell when it's bedtime, Katie."

Rebuked, Katie leaned forward to give her mother a kiss on her cheek. The fumes nearly drove her back.

"I'll call you in the morning, Ma." Turning to Linda she said, "Remember what I said. Anything in the least suspicious, you call."

"Katie," Linda said taking her hand. "I can't thank you enough for all your help."

"Don't be so thankful until you see the bill," Katie joked. "Good night."

JOE KENNEDY WAS WAITING for her when she arrived back at her apartment.

"Hey," she said as she slid between the sheets into his arms. Joe kissed her firmly on the mouth and pulled her on top of him.

"Did you get everything done you wanted to?" he asked as he brushed back her hair.

"Everything I needed to. This is what I want," she said, reaching for him.

"How's your mom's new roomie?" Margo asked the next morning as Katie lugged a computer through the doors of the Black Widow Agency office.

"I just talked to them. Ma had one of her infamous card parties last night and then she and Linda tipped a few back as well. They're both a little groggy this morning," Katie said as she plopped the computer down on Margo's desk.

"You pay for distressed furniture or you just trying to get it for free?" Margo snapped as she looked at the desk.

Katie ignored her and gestured toward the Cybercision Center. "Is Alex back there?"

"No."

"Did she say where she was going?"

"No."

"Did she say when she'd be back?"

"Do I look like a damned gatekeeper to you?" Margo said thrusting her wide hips out. "And if you say I look like a gate, I'll whoop your ass. Besides, that girl is so skinny, she could be standing here right now and we'd never know," she said peeking behind Katie.

Jane Landers was in her office, poring over bank statements from another case. Katie glanced through the glass partition and watched Jane wipe her hand across the back of her neck.

"Janie," she called, "do you know where Alex is?"

"No, Katie." Katie watched as Jane picked up a wet cloth she kept in a small bowl at her desk and wiped her neck with it.

"Is she having hot flashes again?" Katie asked quietly.

"She's got so much damn heat coming off of her I was afraid she was gonna burn the soufflé I just made," Margo said. "I told her she had to stay back."

"Can you try and reach Alex on her cell? I need her to analyze Linda Jordan's computer."

Katie tapped on the counter at Margo's desk impatiently while Margo put her phone on speaker and hit the speed dial button that was automatically programmed to Alex's cell phone. It immediately went into voicemail.

"What about GPS?"

Each of the Black Widow Agency members' cell phones had Global Positioning Systems installed to help locate them in the event of an emergency. Margo brought up a map on her computer that was pre-programmed to locate each of the Black Widow Agency cell phones. Three small red dots appeared in a cluster in one spot.

"It only shows the three of us here," Margo announced. "She must have it shut off."

"Did she take Divinity?"

"That damn bug of hers is still in the Cybercision Center."

KATIE HAD LUGGED LINDA Jordan's computer into the Cybercision Center and started the analysis on it when she heard a slight commotion outside the door. She could hear Margo's raised voice as the door suddenly swung open. Katie quickly blanked the screen in front of her.

"Did I say you could go in there?" Margo said, as she stood in the doorway with her hands thrust on her hips.

Katie watched as Joe Kennedy tried to push past Margo.

"Did I ask?" Joe said, egging her on.

"It would have been the decent thing to do," Margo replied. Looking up and down at Joe Kennedy, she added, "but then again, I don't see why I would expect anything decent from the likes of you. Just because you're carry that badge doesn't mean you can barge in wherever and whenever you like."

"Really?" Joe said jamming his thumbs into his waistband, "because I think it does. Besides, I so look forward to coming here each time and having to listen to you. Aren't you supposed to be like the greeter at Wal-Mart and treat everyone pleasantly?" Glancing past Margo at Katie, he asked, "Isn't that her job?"

"Did you ever watch the people at Wal-Mart kick someone out on their sorry white ass?" Margo retorted.

"How about you call your henchman off before I charge her with disorderly?"

"Who you calling henchman?" Margo asked. "Do I look like any kind of a man to you?" she said thrusting out her chest.

"I guess not," he said. "But I do get distracted by your big…" Joe said, sweeping his eyes to the back side of Margo, "attitude."

Margo took two steps closer to Joe and wagged her finger at him. "You know what? You can just go and kiss my attitude…," she said.

"Okay, enough!" Katie yelled over them both.

"Greeter at Wal-Mart, my damn black ass," Margo said under her breath as she walked out, slamming the door behind her.

Joe shrugged at Katie, feigning innocence, and scanned the room. His eyes fell upon Alexandria's pet tarantula, Divinity. He leaned his tall body over and put his face close to the glass aquarium as Divinity sat quietly in a corner. The spider, sensing his nearness, quickly stuck out a leg in his direction. Joe jumped back.

"Did she get you?" Katie asked.

"Do I look like I can't handle a spider?"

"I'd be careful if I were you, Joe. She hates men."

"Are we talking about the spider or the owner?"

"The jury is still out on that one."

"Believe it or not, Katie," he said sliding onto the counter near her and swiveling her chair around to face him, "I'm here on official police business."

Katie traced her finger on his thigh. "Do you want to frisk me again? I just might be carrying a concealed weapon, you know."

Joe steadied his green eyes on her. "Remind me of that tonight. In the meantime, I'm looking for a missing person. A very famous missing person."

Katie feigned innocence. "What has that to do with me, Joe?"

"I'm told you might know her whereabouts?"

Katie continued to run her finger up Joe's pants leg.

"Come on, Katie, I'm on the job."

"That never used to stop you before. Remember that time in the shooting range? You got off a few good rounds that day, as I recall."

Joe was clearly responding to her touch. "Seriously, Katie, I heard you know where Linda Jordan is."

"Now, who would have told you such a thing?" Katie asked.

"Just someone."

Katie withdrew her hand and pushed her chair back.

"What's the matter?" Joe asked with a confused look on his face.

"We both know who told you, Joe."

"Look, Katie, I still have to deal with her. I'm the shift commander. I have to give out the media log and answer the reporters' questions. That's all it is. Besides," he said, moving closer toward her, "I'm extremely satisfied these days. I have no reason to go elsewhere."

Katie walked over to Divinity's glass tank. The little spider was nestled in a corner, lying very quietly.

"Katie," Joe said, turning her around, "You've got to believe me. There's nothing going on with her."

She shook her head. "Okay, Joe."

"Now about Linda Jordan?"

"Who reported her missing?"

"It was an anonymous call, but they knew enough about her to make it sound legitimate."

"Male or female?"

"Male. Said he was a friend and was supposed to meet with her, but she never showed. Said he heard about the incident on the water yesterday and some of the other threats, and that he was afraid her life was in danger."

"But he didn't give a name?"

"No."

"You didn't get a number?"

Joe reached into his sports coat, took out a slip of paper, and handed it to her. "It's a cell phone registered under the name of John Smith."

Katie looked at the paper and memorized the number. When she went to hand it back to Joe, he grabbed her hand, pulled her close, and put his finger under her chin and lifted it up. "I want you to be very careful with this one, Katie. She's had several close calls already. She could be in a great deal of danger. I mean that."

Katie shrugged and shook her head. "Can't say if we are or we aren't involved, Joe."

"Is that right? Well, maybe I'll have to force it out of you later on," he said as his hands drifted down her neck.

A minute later, the door opened abruptly and Alexandria, noting the two in a hot and heavy embrace, cleared her throat loudly.

KATIE SMOOTHED HER CLOTHES while Joe straightened his tie.

"I'll talk to you later," he said quietly as he headed out.

Katie took out her lipstick and reapplied it. "Nice timing, Alex."

"I heard you were looking for me."

"I was, but you weren't here." Katie waited for a response, but got none. "I started the analysis on Linda Jordan's machine, but I'd like you to finish it."

"Sure."

"And while that's running," she said, scribbling on a note pad, "see if you can trace this number."

A FEW HOURS LATER, the women passed a tray around as they settled into the conference room.

"What are these?" Katie asked as she admired the golden-brown, star-shaped appetizers.

"Butternut squash dumplings with a warm ginger sauce," Margo answered.

"Yumm," Katie said as she popped one in her mouth. "These are incredible, Margo," she said in between chews.

"It's a curse," Margo said.

"What's that?"

"To love your own cooking," she said, swatting her own ample backside. "At least I accept that I'm big, I'm black, and I'm beautiful," she tossed her head back. "You won't see me dying of malnutrition," she said, flashing her brown eyes at Alexandria just as Alexandria declined the tray.

"Anyway," Katie said, as she popped another one in her mouth, "Linda Jordan has officially hired us to keep her, and her manuscript, safe and sound. We need to put together a plan to deliver the manuscript to her publishers."

"Why not just e-mail it to them?" Margo asked.

"We can deliver it by hand to them in an electronic format, but it's too risky to send it electronically. We don't know if someone has put hooks into her or her publisher's computers …"

"They have," Alexandria said. "I found a keystroke logger and some redirectors. It's more than likely whoever infected her system also delivered a payload to her publisher as well."

"Then we'll have to give them the drive with the manuscript in person."

"How?" Margo asked.

"I've got some ideas about that, but in the meantime, Linda is very committed to appearing at a charity event at the Laketon Public Library on Wednesday night. All she has to do is appear. She doesn't have to give any speeches, just be seen, get out of there, and be done."

"Won't that be dangerous for her?" Jane asked.

"Yes, which is why we're not going to let her do it."

"You mean she'll cancel?" Jane asked as she began to wave her hand back and forth, trying to generate a cool breeze.

"Not exactly."

"I'm confused, Katie," Jane said as she lifted her blouse away from her skin and shook it. "If she's committed to being there, but you won't let her be there, then how is she going to …" Jane paused and dropped her blouse back against her damp skin when she saw the look in Katie's eyes. "Oh no, Katie. You couldn't possibly be thinking …"

"Why not? You've fooled them twice already."

"But I don't even look like her. She's much younger than I am. I don't even have red hair. Honestly, Katie, it's impossible."

"It isn't impossible. You can do this, Janie. I know you can. I would never ask you if I didn't think you were up to the task."

"But Katie," Jane said as she began to sweat profusely, "look at me. Really look at me."

"You could pull this off, Janie. You have the same facial structure, you're the same height and build … All you need is a little makeover."

"Makeover? What will you do, go up to a stylist and say, 'Excuse me, could you please make my friend over to look just like Linda Jordan and don't ask why'?"

"I already did."

"I beg your pardon?"

Katie strolled over to the Conference Room door and whipped it open. Marcus and Antoine stood opposite each other leaning casually against the door frame. Antoine clutched a hair dryer while Marcus held a makeup case.

"Hello, darlings. The Sachet & Sashay Salon is now open!" Marcus announced.

"A LITTLE BLING, JANE, darling, and you'll be a best-seller," said Marcus as he casually flipped through the pages of a fashion magazine while Antoine worked on her hair.

"Bling?" Jane asked, with a panicked look on her face. "What is bling? Is that a chemical?"

Katie rolled her eyes. "No, Janie. Bling means glam, sparkle."

"Oh. Well, I suppose I'll need a lot of this bling stuff to pull this off."

"She's not kidding," Marcus muttered under his breath. Margo reached over and jabbed her brother in the arm.

"Don't worry, Janie. Linda Jordan doesn't exactly exude a lot of bling. Besides, you're in excellent hands," Katie said.

Antoine, Marcus' partner in business and in life, stood by an entire counter filled with products and solutions.

"Fortunately," Antoine said, "I kept all of my equipment from when I had my salon in Boston, and even more fortunately, our latest BeGay order just arrived."

"BeGay?" Katie asked.

"It's an on-line auction site exclusively for gay people," Antoine explained as he took the towel off Jane's damp hair.

"Oh."

Marcus lowered the magazine he was looking at. "Surely you cyber charlatans have heard of BeGay?" Turning to Alexandria, he said, "It's on the Internet, for heaven's sakes. I thought you knew about everything on the Internet."

Alexandria shrugged.

"We don't just bid on things, darlings, we critique them first," Marcus explained.

"That's called Bitch Bidding," Antoine said with a smile, as he sprayed Jane's hair with a hair product.

Katie laughed. "Now this I've got to see," she said. She motioned Alexandria to bring up the site on the big screen. The graphics were incredible.

"Queer Gear?" Margo asked, reading from the content list.

"Personal items, sister darling," Marcus explained, "like clothing, hair products, etc. It takes a lot to look this good," he added, patting his own jet-black hair.

"Homo, Sweet Homo?" Alexandria asked.

"Items for house and home."

"The Outhouse?" Katie asked.

"Entertaining ideas, as in coming out parties, commitment ceremonies, and the like."

"The Gender Blender?" Margo asked.

"Items for the kitchen. Honestly, girlfriends, this is not rocket science."

ANTOINE TOOK A LONG time cutting Jane's hair in Linda Jordan's lightly curled, swept-away style. Katie realized how difficult it must be for him to correct such a botched cut. Everyone suspected that Jane, in her own frugal way, had been cutting her own hair for some time in a simple pageboy style. Antoine layered the back and much to everyone's surprise, Jane's hair began to curl on its own. Next, Antoine rolled her hair in strips of foil.

Marcus passed by with a tall, blue drink in his hand.

"What you got there, Marcus, a Viagra Straight Up?" Katie asked.

Marcus peered at her over his glass and smiled. "Very clever, Katarina, darling," he said as he slowly sipped the blue concoction. "Actually, it's a delicious blend of Blue Curacao, Vodka, Crème de Cacao, Rum cream liqueur, and ice-cream…" He waited patiently for her to ask the question.

"Wow, a regular health smoothie," Katie said. Relenting to him, she finally asked, "Okay, so what is it called?"

Marcus peered at Antoine as he replied, "a Sexy, Blue-Eyed Boy." Antoine grinned and went back to working on Jane's hair.

Katie sat down and picked up a fashion magazine from the table. She wore her navy-blue blazer and tan khakis over a white T-shirt, and flat blue pumps with no socks, revealing the small tattoo of their trademark black widow spider with a red rose on its back, on her inner right ankle.

"Katarina, darling," Marcus said, peering at her over his drink, "when are you going to come out?"

Everyone in the room, including Margo, who was flipping through the magazines, stopped what they were doing and looked over.

"I beg your pardon?" Katie laughed.

"Darling," Marcus said, approaching her, "I ooze more femininity in my sleep." He touched the lapels of her blazer. Katie swatted his hands away.

"Hands off, Marcus, unless you mean it," Katie said. "You know I like to be comfortable."

"There's nothing wrong with being comfortable, Katie," Jane said from the chair. Katie wasn't so sure she appreciated support coming from a sixty-year-old woman who lived for elastic-waisted everything.

"And that truck you drive," Marcus commented.

"It's not a truck, Marcus. It's an SUV," Katie explained.

"As in Seriously Ugly Vehicle," Marcus frowned.

"This is New England. You know, blizzards? Four-wheel drive? Helloooo?"

Marcus set his blue drink down and slipped behind Katie. Ignoring her order not to touch her, he pulled her thick, curly reddish-blonde hair away from her face.

"Comfortable went out in 1985," he said, leaning over. "You could start by doing something with this mop," he said as he twisted her hair up and pulled it back on her head. "Antoine could do you next while he has all of his equipment out. And trust me, he knows how to work his equipment."

"Marcus!" his sister said in an outraged tone. "Don't be so damn rude. Leave her alone." Hesitantly, she added, "You know what though, girlfriend? It kind of does look good pulled up and back like that. Makes you look younger."

Katie, who was painfully about to turn thirty-nine, did not appreciate the "younger" comment.

"Really, Katarina, darling, when was the last time you went to an actual stylist instead of some beauty school dropout named 'Crystal,' or 'Jodi,' spelled with an 'i'?" Marcus asked.

Katie grimaced, knowing how close he was to the truth, but she couldn't see the point of spending seventy-five dollars on a salon cut when all she needed was a straight trim in the back which could be done by anyone who could hold a pair of scissors.

"And these," Marcus said, releasing her hair and touching her breasts with no hesitation whatsoever, "are a gift from God that should not be squirreled away." He came around, picked up his drink with one hand and a thick copy of *Vogue* with the other. "Now this," he said, flipping the glossy pages around to face her, "would look divine on you. It flows. It's Roberto Cavalli. You have the height and the lovely white meat to carry it off."

Katie looked at the picture. "It looks like she has a tree growing up her legs," she said observing the fabric with a wild print of vines and branches.

Marcus shook his head and turned the pages, "Here. Carolina Herrera. Very hot. Very much the new black."

"I thought you said gay was the new black."

Katie looked at the dress with the halter top and photos of silhouetted swimmers all over it. "A halter top on these shoulders?" she asked shaking her head. "I don't think so. Besides, is that supposed to be swimwear or dinner wear or what?"

Marcus threw his hands up. "Katarina, darling, you're a fashion abomination."

"I know, but I like to be comfortable when I'm working."

"One of these days, my fashion faux pas, I'll have my way with you."

"Take a number."

"ANY LUCK ON TRACING that cell phone?" Katie asked Alexandria as they all waited in the conference room for Antoine to finish with Jane.

Alexandria, who was petting Divinity, did not look at Katie when she said, "No."

Marcus suddenly whipped open the Black Widow Agency conference room door. "Ladies … and gentleman," he threw toward Katie as she flipped him off, "may I present to you, Miss Linda Jordan."

Mouths dropped open as Jane swung around from behind Marcus.

"Sweet Jesus," Margo said.

"Mary, Mother of God," said Katie.

Alexandria just stared.

THE TRANSFORMATION WAS ASTOUNDING. Jane's hair, now a lovely auburn shade, was cut in the same exact style as Linda Jordan's. Her eyebrows had been dyed darker and reshaped in a straight line across her brow. Katie picked up her copy of *The Franklin Cure*, flipped it to the back cover and held it up.

"Amazing. This can work," she said looking up and down Jane. "There's only one thing missing."

"It will be here tomorrow," Alexandria said.

11

Gracelyn MacDougal appeared the minute Katie crossed the threshold of Shamrock Shores. Her eyes swept to the two large photo albums tucked under Katie's arms.

"Hello, Mrs. MacDougal," Katie called as Gracelyn fell into step beside her.

"Hello, Miss Mahoney."

Katie kept walking, but Gracelyn stayed with her.

"If you don't mind, I'd like to speak to you about your mother, for a moment," she said.

Katie paused. "If you don't mind, Mrs. MacDougal, I'm a little pressed for time."

"I'm concerned about her."

"Oh?"

"I knocked on her door last night to return a knitting needle of hers and it took her some time to get to the door and she seemed, well ... reluctant to greet me." Looking around the room to make sure no one else could hear them, Gracelyn lowered her voice when she said, "I thought perhaps Mr. Collins was, you know ... visiting ... but he was in the Emerald Room watching television. I hope there's nothing wrong."

Katie thought quickly. "She ... she's ... a bit ... irregular sometimes."

"Ahhh ..." Gracelyn said nodding. "Many of our residents have the same issue from time to time. Of course. I understand. Perhaps I can offer some home remedies. Tell her to call me and I can make a few suggestions ..."

"That's so sweet of you," Katie said. "I'll be sure to let her know."

Katie was almost away when Gracelyn said, "Photo albums?"

Katie cleared her throat. "She's still working on the family scrapbook. The more the merrier ..."

KATIE KNOCKED TWO TIMES, waited, then knocked three times. Her mother opened the door promptly. Linda Jordan sat at her mother's table, her fingers flying across the keyboard. When she saw Katie, she quickly undid the chain around her neck, took the thumb drive out and saved the contents of what was on her computer to the portable drive.

"Hello, sweetie," Molly Mahoney said, leaning forward to give her daughter a peck on the cheek. Her eyes narrowed when she saw the photo albums tucked under Katie's arms. "You didn't get to go shopping?" she asked, somewhat disappointed.

Katie set the photo albums down and opened them to reveal two see-through plastic bags filled with a golden colored liquid.

"What are those?"

"They're called bladders. They each hold a gallon's worth."

"A gallon's worth each?" Looking back at Linda Jordan, Molly winked and said, "We're good for tonight, Linda."

Linda laughed, got up and stretched. "But where's yours, Molly?" she asked squeezing her arm as she passed by. "If you ladies don't mind, I worked through the night. I'm going to take a little nap."

KATIE WAITED UNTIL THE guestroom door shut before she retrieved the clean bottles Molly had stored in the cabinet and began to refill them.

"So how's it going, Ma?"

"You know Katie, at first I couldn't imagine anyone wanting to be holed up in a room with me all this time. But the funny thing is, we're quite companionable and Linda doesn't seem to mind the seclusion at all. Personally, I think I'd go batty after the first couple of days, but it doesn't seem to bother her at all. She says it's a writer's life. She works for hours and hours and then sleeps, eats occasionally, and then does it all over again. I had no idea that writing was such hard work and so exhausting."

"Hey Ma," Katie said glancing at the shut door, "you do realize you're involved in making history here."

"Oh, I don't know about that, Katie."

"Does she ever talk about the sequel?"

"Not much. We talk about other things, though. Did you know she became a writer when her husband, who was a teacher, had an affair with one of his students? They divorced and she needed to find a way to make money."

"I think I read that somewhere."

"He sued her to try and get half the profits of *The Franklin Cure* when it became a best-seller, but the court said no. Can you imagine? The poor thing."

"One thing she's not now, Ma, is poor."

"Well, I'm happy for her. And she's established a charity, the Linda Jordan Foundation, to assist those in need."

"I didn't know that."

SOMETIMES CLIENTS WHO SOUGHT the Black Widow Agency's services were in great need. Katie treated all equally and charged on a sliding scale based on the ability to pay, a policy that sometimes flustered Jane Landers, who found it disconcerting to not be able to project their income month by month. But many of their clients were of means and more than made up for the occasional destitute client. Katie had sometimes waived their fees entirely if a woman was truly in need. Having a tie to Linda Jordan's foundation could be an interesting opportunity to help more women who crossed their paths.

"BY THE WAY, MA, you might want to go out a little more. Mrs. MacDougal cornered me and said she's worried about you because you haven't been out much."

"Oh dear. What did you say to her?"

"That you were full of shit."

"Katie!"

"Sorry, but I had to think of something. Oh, and by the way, don't be surprised if she shows up with prune pie and extra pulp orange juice."

"Honestly, Katie, was that really necessary?"

KATIE WAS POURING THE remains into the last bottle when there was a small tap on her mother's door. She nearly spilled the contents as she quickly closed the bottle and tossed the empty bladders into the trash. They both glanced anxiously at the guest bedroom door. Katie signaled to her mother that the coast was clear.

Molly opened the door. There stood Timothy Collins, almost at attention in the doorway.

"Hello, Timothy," Molly said, as she held her hand out to him in what seemed, to Katie, such an old-fashioned gesture.

"Dear Molly, how are you," he said as he reached forward, took her hand and patted it. Glancing up, he saw Katie standing by the sink.

"Hi, Mr. Collins. How are you?"

"She said, how are you?" Molly repeated. "That's my girl, Katie."

"I heard her," Timothy replied. He nodded his head very formally. Katie gave a wave back.

"I'd invite you in, Timothy," Molly began, "but I have company."

"We've been worried about you, Molly. No one has seen much of you the last couple of days."

"I … I've been …" Molly flustered.

"I've had her tied up going over our family history," Katie said as she sat down in front of Linda Jordan's laptop and pretended to type. "Always nice to know your ancestors. Ma, why don't you go with Mr. Collins and the others and visit with them since they've been so worried about you?"

"But won't our ..."

"Our history will still be here when you get back," Katie said. "Go on."

"I'll just grab my sweater. It's in the guest ...," Molly began to say but quickly caught herself. "On the other hand, it's plenty warm."

Timothy and Molly were halfway out the door when the guest bedroom door suddenly flung open and Linda Jordan stepped out. "I was about to fall asleep and thought of the perfect way to end chapter twenty ..."

They all looked at each other as one by one, they realized the dilemma they were in.

Katie quickly went round to the door and yanked Timothy Collins and her mother back in.

"Oh dear," Molly said under her breath.

"Mr. Collins," Katie said shutting the door, "this is a friend of ours ..."

"I know who she is," Timothy said, looking between the three women, and waiting for an explanation.

"Shit," Katie said very quietly.

"So you see then, Mr. Collins," Katie said as they sat at Molly's small table, "as a police officer, I'm sure you can appreciate the situation we have here. Miss Jordan is only safe if her whereabouts are kept hidden."

"I didn't get to be captain of the state police by running my mouth off."

"I appreciate that, sir," she threw in for extra measure.

"In fact," Timothy said, "it's probably a good thing you told me. I retired with my service revolver, you know. It's a Smith & Wesson short barrel thirty-eight."

"As long as no one knows she's here, I really don't think that will be necessary."

"We'll keep those bastards at bay!" he said thumping the table. Turning to Linda and Molly, he said, "Pardon my French, ladies."

"Again, I really don't think that will be necessary, but I do appreciate the offer and all of your years of dedicated service to law enforcement."

"It's a lousy job, but someone has to do it."

"The best thing for everyone's safety is to keep up normal appearances, so why don't the two of you head out and mingle for a bit?"

"What do you say, Molly?" Timothy Collins said glancing at his watch. "It's almost time for *Adam-12*."

"You watch *Adam-12*?" Katie asked.

"Only police show that ever got it right!" Timothy shouted. "Not like any of these shows today that don't know their arrests from their affidavits."

They shuffled out arm in arm.

"I didn't realize your mother had a special friend," Linda observed after they left. "I hope I haven't kept them from seeing each other."

"I don't believe you have. And if my gut instinct is right, your secrets are still very safe."

Linda Jordan began to walk back toward the guest room, but stopped and turned.

"Katie," she began, "I was talking to Molly last night. She told me about you and Captain Kennedy… She seems very happy for you both. Says he's a good man."

"He is, and I'm sorry for not telling you myself. It was… personal."

"Of course."

KATIE WALKED BACK INTO the Cybercision Center, looking for Alexandria, and noticed one of the computer screens was at a site for a company called "TBI Pharmaceuticals." Katie noticed several other search engines open, all with the same company name entered in them. Shrugging, she kept going on to the kitchen and through to the adjoining offices of Sachet & Sashay. She heard lowered voices coming from one of the rooms Marcus and Antoine used to entertain clients.

ANTOINE WAS SITTING FORWARD in a chair, while Alexandria sat on the coffee table directly in front of him. Both were leaning closely toward each other and if Katie didn't know any better, she could have sworn they were holding hands, but both pulled away when she said, "Hey, Alex." There was something in their body posture that made Katie feel as if she had intruded on something very private. She saw

Alexandria's shoulders stiffen and her frozen reserve reappear as she slowly turned to face Katie.

"Yes?"

"Margo told me you were here. I need you back so we can work out a game plan for tomorrow night." She cleared her throat. "Sorry if I interrupted."

"It's okay," Antoine said. "We were just discussing some changes to the Sachet & Sashay web site."

Katie didn't believe a word he said.

"ARE YOU SURE I won't have to make a speech?" Jane asked nervously.

"Positive. All you need to do is appear."

"But what if the reporters ask me questions? What if someone asks me to sign copies of their books?"

"The reporters have been told this is a nonspeaking appearance. You can just walk by them with no comment. And there won't be any book signing. All you have to do is step up, cut the ribbon, have some pictures taken and get out of there."

"But surely they'll know it isn't the real Linda Jordan," Jane said.

"Not necessarily. It will be outdoors so it would be perfectly appropriate for you to have on a hat and sunglasses."

Jane wiped nervously at her neck with a white handkerchief.

"I'll be right behind you the whole time, Janie. We'll all be there," she said, looking between Alexandria and Margo. "It will be a piece of cake. All you have to do is wear this," she said handing her an identical silver fob to the one that Linda Jordan wore. Jane took the fob and opened it. Instead of the thumb drive, it had a small device that looked like a tiny remote.

"What's this?" Jane asked.

"A GPS receiver."

"But I thought you said you would be right there."

"We will, but it's always good to use whatever tools we have as backup."

"KATIE," MARGO BEGAN AS soon as Jane went back to her office. "I've been thinking, isn't this dangerous for Jane? I mean, someone did try to make Linda Jordan shark bait the other day."

Alexandria raised her eyebrows and looked at Katie, waiting for her to respond. "She does have a point," she said quietly.

Katie sighed. "I thought about that too, but look at this," she said as she took the laptop from Alexandria's lap. She quickly typed in Linda Jordan's name and the word "appearing" in a search engine and came up with dozens of hits. "If someone had actually wanted to do her harm, they have had ample opportunity to do so. While she may be considered "reclusive," she has made a number of public appearances over the last year, particularly in the Seacoast area. I don't think they're after Linda at all. I just think someone knows if they can get their hands on that manuscript, it is worth two million dollars. By the way, Alex, did you have any luck with that cell number?"

"You already asked me and I told you no."

LATER THAT EVENING, KATIE laid her head on Joe's chest and brushed her fingers through his chest hair as he ran his hands softly up and down her back.

"That was very nice," she said, as she closed her eyes.

"It just keeps getting better and better, doesn't it?"

"At this rate, think about how good it will be by the time we reach my mother's age."

Joe gave a small laugh and twirled his fingers round in circles around her back. Katie let out a deep, satisfied sigh.

"Speaking of your mother, how is she doing these days?"

"She's fine," Katie said groggily. "Still best friends with her buddy, Jack."

Joe laughed. "I was thinking of stopping by this week to see her. I haven't seen her in a while. Maybe I can find time on Thursday ..."

Katie immediately lifted her head up. "You can't."

"Why not?"

"She's ... not feeling well."

"You just said she was fine."

"She is, but she isn't. I mean, it's ... it's kind of a personal thing."

Joe looked at her curiously. "What kind of a personal thing?"

"She's ... she's ... you know ... bound."

Joe tapped her on the butt. "Prune juice," he said. "Works every time."

No one was more surprised by the size of the crowd at the library ribbon cutting ceremony than Katie herself. From the limo, Jane looked anxiously at the throngs of people packed three-deep on along the ribbon. Katie immediately spotted Joe on the cutting side of the ribbon. He was scanning the crowd from behind aviator-style sunglasses. She saw Margo in the crowd near the ribbon, taking pictures with a digital camera, as well as several officers, some in uniform, some in plainclothes, dispersed throughout the crowd.

"Oh, dear," Jane said, as she began to fan herself. "I don't think I can do this."

"We'll be in and out, Janie," Katie said reassuringly.

"But look at all those people."

"Listen to me, Janie. You've done undercover work before. You're an experienced professional." Katie lifted the leg of Jane's lavender pants suit and pointed to the tattoo of the black widow spider on her inner ankle. "That is a symbol of your strength and your dedication to the job. You wouldn't have it if you weren't capable of doing this."

"Do you really think so?"

"I know so. Come on. Let's give this crowd a show," she said, offering a hand to Jane as Alexandria, who was dressed in a black suit and acting as their chauffeur for the evening, opened the door of the limousine.

"Linda! Linda!" the crowd cheered as Jane emerged. At first, Katie was afraid she was going to turn right around and jump back in the limo, but Jane looked curiously at the crowds clamoring for her attention, set her shoulders back, lifted her chin, and gave a big wave that set the crowd breaking into a huge round of applause.

"They like me," she shouted into Katie's ear.

"Of course they like you," Katie said. "They adore you."

"Miss Jordan! Miss Jordan! When will the sequel to *The Franklin Cure* be finished?" one reporter shouted.

"Miss Jordan, is it true there's a two-million-dollar bounty on the sequel?"

"Have you given it a title yet?"

"Miss Jordan has no comment," Katie told them as she placed a firm hand on Jane's back and pushed her through the crowds toward the ribbon where the library director, a small woman with bad teeth; the library trustees, who all seemed to be over seventy; and the town manager, all stood.

"Miss Jordan, it is an honor," said the town manager, a large man with a receding hairline and a not-so-receding waistline.

"The honor is mine," Jane said, shaking his hand.

Joe Kennedy spied Katie and began to work his way toward her.

"You didn't tell me you'd be here," he said, as he arrived beside her, with a look that said he was not pleased.

"Surprise, surprise," Katie replied. "Sorry, Joe, but you know how it is. Work is work."

"I guess. Still, it would have been nice to notify the local authorities. Just as a courtesy."

"I was going to notify a certain authority last night," Katie said, lowering her voice, "but he distracted me for hours."

Joe gave her a small nod and turned back to study the crowds.

"Ladies and gentlemen," the library director began, as she pulled out a small sheet of paper and unfolded it. "This outdoor reading area and park represents the culmination of our long-range strategic goals, which have been on-going for eight years now. I want to thank the board of trustees for their continued support of this project." She waited for the applause to die down. "But it is a special honor, in fact a privilege, to celebrate this auspicious occasion with a woman who has been named by *The New Yorker* magazine as, and I quote, "one of the most significant writers of our day, if not our century." Ladies and gentlemen, it is my honor and pleasure to introduce to you the prime supporter of this project, Miss Linda Jordan."

There was a tremendous thunder of applause as Jane was pushed toward the podium and the realization that they expected her to make a speech dawned on both Katie and Jane at the same time. The look of confidence that Jane had worn moments ago evaporated as sheer panic set in. Katie broke away from Joe, grabbed Jane by the arm, and leaned down toward her ear. Beads of sweat were beginning to form around the base of Jane's neck.

"It's okay, Janie. Very few people have ever heard Linda Jordan speak. Just say something nice and we'll get the hell out of here."

"But Katie," Jane gulped. "I can't."

"You're a Black Widow, damn it," Katie said sternly. "A black widow can eat its mate and spin a web at the same time. You can make a lousy speech. Turn and smile to them. Pretend little Mary-Jane is out there and make her proud."

Jane wiped at her neck and nodded. She plastered a fake smile on her face and approached the podium. The crowd went wild. "Linda! Linda!" they chanted. Katie watched as Jane's eyes swept across the throngs and her plastic smile was replaced by a genuine one. Jane looked back at Katie and winked.

"As you all know," Jane began as the crowd hushed, "I love a strong ending and I can't think of a better ending to a long-range plan than to dedicate this lovely area to the pursuit of reading." The crowd broke out in applause but hushed as Jane spoke again. "I want to thank the Laketon Public Library for their invitation to participate in this event. Thank you all for your support," Jane said as she gave a final wave and stepped back away from the microphone.

Katie grabbed her by the arm, pulled her close and said, "Do me a favor will you?"

"What's that?"

"Give yourself a raise when we get back to the office," Katie said squeezing her arm.

They waited for the speeches to end before turning back toward the limo.

"Miss Jordan!" the reporters began as they pushed forward, "will the sequel be as controversial as the first?"

"Miss Jordan, how do you respond to the families of patients who died trying *The Franklin Cure*?"

"Keep walking," Katie said firmly as she led Jane away.

"Are you really Linda Jordan?" one lone voice rang out.

Katie glanced over her shoulder into the eyes of Chelsea Mattox as she stood, arms folded across her perky breasts, watching them steadily as they passed by. Katie could feel Jane losing her strength and almost had to hold her up as the reporters followed them to the limo.

Spotting Alexandria, Katie said quietly, "Get us the hell out of here. Fast."

As they were about to enter the limo, Katie suddenly felt something pull her off-balance and found herself being shoved down to the pavement. Looking up, she saw a man in his mid-thirties with a very long salt and pepper beard lunge toward Jane. He yanked at the chain on her neck. Katie heard Jane scream as the straw hat went flying. Jane clutched at her neck while the man yanked at the chain and tried to wrestle it off of her. Katie got back on her feet and with all her strength, slammed her elbow into the man's kidneys. At the delivery of the blow, the man loosened his grasp enough to spin toward her as she reached for the gun she was carrying on her belt. Before she could draw her weapon, Joe was behind the man and grabbing him in a headlock. Katie took the opportunity to deliver a pointed knee in the direction of the man's groin. He crumbled to the ground.

"Go, go, go!" Katie shouted as she shoved Jane into the back of the limo. Alexandria slammed the car door, jumped into the driver's seat, and sped off.

JANE WAS DRENCHED IN sweat. Katie got her a cool cloth from the wet bar which Jane gratefully took and wrapped around her neck.

"Are you okay?"

"I … I don't know."

"It's all over with. You did great."

"I don't know, Katie. That man could have killed us."

"He was just grabbing for the gold, or in this case, the silver. Relax. You're safe now. You won't have to be Linda Jordan ever again."

"I'd better not," Jane said as she took the hat, the sunglasses and the silver fob off. "I've had quite enough of being Linda Jordan, thank you. Between that man and that reporter … How in the world did she know I wasn't real?"

"She's like a wasp. A damn pesky wasp that's always buzzing around and getting in our faces. A wasp I'll someday get rid of."

"Wasp or no wasp, they both gave me quite a fright," Jane said as she clutched the wet cloth to her throat.

"She should be the one who is frightened. She ought to know that the black widow spider and wasps are natural enemies …"

They gathered later at the Black Widow Agency offices.

"Okay, thanks, Joe," Katie said into the phone. Lowering her voice, she said, "I am, too. We'll have to discuss that particular case in-depth later, if you don't mind."

"And then he tried to get the silver thing, but Captain Kennedy showed up out of nowhere and grabbed him from behind. Then Katie kneed him in a particularly delicate spot," Jane was telling Margo as Katie joined them in the kitchen.

"That's our Katie. Always busting somebody's balls," Margo observed.

"Seems that way, doesn't it?" Katie replied. "That was Joe. The guy who tried to grab your fob was just a low-life who heard about the bounty. He's got a lengthy history of petty thefts. They'll charge him with simple assault, but Joe wanted us to know that he wasn't any serious threat."

"I guess that's good news," Jane said.

"Sort of," Katie said.

"What did you want them to do, whoop Jane's ass?" Margo asked. "That'd make you feel better, would it?"

"No, of course not. I just mean it doesn't get us any closer to who is a serious threat." Looking at the three women, she said, "In any case, we need to celebrate a successful mission and Jane's good work."

"I'm already on it," Margo said as she took out what had become their tradition upon the successful completion of their mission, a celebratory dessert.

"Heavens," Jane said eyeing the bowls, "what is that?"

"It's a special trifle I made with brandy-soaked ladyfingers, pastry cream, and homemade chocolate sauce," Margo explained. "It's got all four food groups—chocolate, alcohol, cream, and cake."

"Here's to the four food groups," Katie said as they clinked bowls.

KATIE SNAPPED HER FINGERS and paced back and forth across the conference room floor.

"You keep pacing like that," Margo complained, "and you're going to wear a hole in that damn rug."

Katie kept walking. "The manuscript is due to be delivered to Ryan & Rogers at four p.m. tomorrow in Portville. Linda insists on handing it over herself."

"Why?"

"She said handing the completed manuscript over is like handing your baby over and she wants to see that it gets there safe and sound. We need to figure out the best way to do that."

"Why not just drive her up in the back of the van?" Margo asked.

"Logically that would make sense, but ..."

"Katie," Jane interrupted, "Margo has a point. If she's out of sight then what's the danger?"

Katie glanced at Alexandria for a moment before answering.

"I don't know. I just have a strange feeling ..."

"What kind of a strange feeling?" Margo asked.

"You know the black widow is able to tell when something is approaching because she spins her web and senses the vibrations whenever something comes near?"

"Yes."

"I want to know what's trying to get across the web ..."

ALEXANDRIA REACHED FOR HER ringing cell phone, glanced at it for a moment and tucked it back in her pocket. Without saying a word to anyone, she rose.

"Where are you going?" Katie asked.

"Out," was all she offered as she walked out the door.

"WAS THAT A BLACK widow spider you were talkin' about a minute ago?" Margo asked. "Or a black-haired weirdo, 'cause I think we got one of those stuck in our little web."

"She has been acting a bit odd lately," Jane added. "I'm concerned about her, Katie."

"She's a grown woman who has her own life and her own world," Katie replied. "We have to respect that. Just because she's ..."

"Weird?" Margo threw out.

"I was going to say, 'private.'"

"I know about 'private,'" Margo said. "'Private' is a nice way of saying 'weird.'"

"Whatever. It's her business."

"I thought her business was this business."

"Look, it is frustrating, I admit, to not know what she does and where she goes, but it is what it is," Katie said as she went over and poured herself a glass of scotch.

Just then, the phone rang.

"I'll get it," Jane said as she picked up the receiver.

"Good morning, Black Widow Agency, may I help you? Yes. May I ask … I see. Is everything all right? Oh dear. Oh no. Hold on," Jane said as she thrust the phone toward Katie.

"What is it?"

"It's Mrs. MacDougal from Shamrock Shores. She says your mother and Linda Jordan have just been kidnapped."

"I CANNOT BELIEVE, SIMPLY cannot believe, that Linda Jordan was here," Gracelyn MacDougal said very excitedly as she and Katie walked hurriedly through the halls of Shamrock Shores. "I had no idea your mother even knew her."

"It's a long story, Mrs. MacDougal, but now's not the time to explain. Tell me again, everything you saw."

"I was just going to bring your mother some fresh prunes for … you know … her difficulty … when I looked out my office window and saw a man in a dark cap and sunglasses out in the parking lot, pushing your mother and Linda Jordan into a car. Your mother had her knitting bag with her. The man kept one hand in his jacket pocket the whole time. Then Mr. Collins appeared out of nowhere and shouted something to the man and the man grabbed him and shoved him in, too. They struggled for a minute but the man seemed much stronger. His hand was shoved deep in his pocket and he kept waving it around at them. Oh dear," Mrs. MacDougal said. "You don't suppose he had a gun or anything, do you? I don't understand what's happening. Why would Linda Jordan be at Shamrock Shores? Why did this man push them in the car like that?"

"I'll explain everything another time. I appreciate you not calling the police right away. I'll take care of notifying them. Can you tell me anything about the car? Did it have New Hampshire plates?"

"Yes, I think so."

"Was it a dark car or a light car?"

"Dark. Dark green, actually."

"Sedan?"

"Yes. New."

"MOTHER OF MARY, WHAT is going on, Katie?" Mrs. Timmons asked panting as she and Mrs. McAfee caught up with Katie in the hallway. "We heard that Molly, Timothy Collins, and Linda Jordan were all kidnapped by a gang."

"Not exactly, but they have been taken away. I need you two," she said sternly to them both, "to tell me the truth. Did either of you know that Linda Jordan was here?"

The two women looked between each other and dropped their heads to the ground.

"We were just so worried about Molly," Mrs. Timmons began. "She wasn't coming out and our ..." Mrs. Timmons paused, looked over her shoulder toward Gracelyn MacDougal's office and lowered her voice, "... card games stopped, if you know what I mean."

"I understand."

"So we decided to make sure she was okay. We knocked a couple of times and waited, but there was no answer, so we knocked again..."

The secret knock, Katie thought to herself.

"And she opened the door with a big smile, thinking it was you, but it was us, and then we looked over and there was Linda Jordan, *the* Linda Jordan, sitting at Molly's kitchen table, typing away."

"It was so exciting," Mrs. McAfee added. "We've never had a famous guest here before."

"And by any chance did either of you mention the fact that Linda Jordan was here to anyone else?"

The two women looked down at the tiled floor again.

"Only to my Boyd," Mrs. McAfee finally said. "But he's a police officer and completely trustworthy," she quickly added.

Yeah, right, Katie thought to herself as she recalled the many times in her career when items of value were stolen right out from each others' police lockers.

"And I may have mentioned it to the receptionist at my doctor's office," Mrs. Timmons confessed, "but she was sitting right there reading *The Franklin Cure*. It just slipped out."

"We would never do anything to hurt Molly, you know that," Mrs. McAfee said.

"I know," Katie replied.

"Is there anything we can do? We're so worried about them."

"Not unless there's anything else you can tell me."

Katie was about to walk out when Mrs. Timmons said, "I don't know if it matters or not, but your mother was on the community computer this morning."

"The community computer?"

"It's in the Hibernian Room. It's for all the residents to use. It has that Internet and everything. It was unusual to see her on it, so I asked her what she was doing and she whispered to me that she had to send an e-mail out for Linda Jordan."

"Did she say what it was about?"

"No, not that I recall."

"Show me this computer."

"I'll get it back to you as soon as I can," Katie said as Grace-lyn MacDougal cornered her. Katie clutched the laptop Linda Jordan used under one arm and the community computer under the other.

"But it's the only one we have …"

"Look," Katie said eyeing the ancient computer. "I'll replace it with a brand new one, okay? But I need this machine and I need it now."

"A new one? Well, I suppose."

Katie hauled the computer into the Black Widow Agency offices. "Please tell me Alex is here," she said to Margo as she set the computer down heavily on her desk.

Margo jumped at the loud thump and shook her head.

Marcus and Antoine were sitting around, sipping drinks and reading interior decorator magazines.

"You may not care about what you look like, Katarina," Marcus admonished, "but that desk does. It could be an antique some-day."

"Ask me if I care," Katie shot back. Marcus raised his eyebrow as his sister waved him off.

"Did you find out anything?" Jane asked.

"My mother, Linda Jordan, and their friend Mr. Collins were all kidnapped, possibly at gunpoint, and it may have something to do with an e-mail my mother sent, but I can't friggin' tell until I get this computer analyzed, and once again, Alex isn't here. Damn her, of all times," Katie said as she slammed her hand on the desk. "I need her now!"

"I know where she is," a lone voice said.

Katie whipped around. "What?"

"No one is supposed to know," Antoine said.

"How do you? ... Never mind. Where is she?"

"I swore I would never tell ..."

"Antoine, three lives are in danger. I need Alex to get into that e-mail and see what it says. You have to tell me."

"Sounds to me, sweet peaches," Marcus said, rubbing his partner's forearm, "that you have no choice."

Antoine nodded, leaned forward, and whispered into Katie's ear. Katie grabbed her jacket and bolted out the door.

15

Katie whipped open the front entrance door of the Laketon General Children's Hospital and was surprised to see that it looked more like the lobby of a comfortable hotel. A large, wood-paneled information desk wrapped around the center of a waiting room filled with overstuffed leather chairs and coffee tables stacked with magazines. At the end, a coffee bar offered a variety of flavors, along with a sign that read, "Please help yourself." To the left was a grand piano with potted plants all around it. An older woman with pure white hair and a volunteer jacket played a smooth jazz tune and smiled at Katie as she walked in. She went up to the information desk, spoke to another volunteer, and bolted for the elevators.

The atmosphere changed as soon as she got off the third floor. Despite the cheerful wallpaper of fish smiling and waving their fins as they swam through the ocean alongside whales and dolphins, the distinctive smell of antiseptic filled the hallways.

Katie looked around, but wasn't sure which way to go. A white-haired man wearing a white coat walked by. The stethoscope slung around his neck had a little stuffed koala attached to it.

"Excuse me," Katie said, stopping him, "can you tell me where the oncology ward is?"

"Yes, of course," the gentleman said, "it's just around the corner to the left. You can't miss it. Are you looking for someone in particular?"

"Yes, her name is Alexandria Axelrod."

The man smiled. "Of course, Alex. Are you a friend of hers?"

"We work together. I mean we work together, and yes, we're friends." Katie put out her hand. "I'm Katie Mahoney."

The gentleman shook her hand. "She's mentioned you to me several times. I'm Dr. Davis. She's in the ward," he said pointing.

"The ward?"

"With the other patients."

"Other patients?"

"We're so lucky to have her," Dr. Davis said smiling. "Many of our former patients leave and never come back. You can't blame them, really. It takes someone with tremendous courage to return, but it gives us all much-needed hope. Good-bye," he said as he walked off, leaving a completely dumbfounded Katie standing in the middle of the hall.

THE ONCOLOGY WARD OF the Laketon General Children's Hospital was specifically designed with glass walls so families of the patients could see all that went on without always having to stay inside the treatment area. Private sitting rooms were also available to the patients and their families when they needed time to rest, break down, or pray for a miracle.

Katie stood outside the large wall of glass and watched as the surreal scene unfolded in front of her. Alexandria's short black hair stood out dramatically against the sea of bald heads. The children were huddled around her as she moved a mouse over a big screen and showed them how to navigate around the Internet. Katie watched in shock as Alexandria turned to one of the children, reached over, picked up his hand which was attached to an IV pole, and placed it on the mouse. As the young man moved the mouse, she gently rubbed his back, encouraging him on. The child successfully found what he was looking for and Alexandria clapped her hands. The other children clamored to be next. One young boy tapped Alexandria on the shoulder and Katie watched with unbelieving eyes as Alexandria scooped the young child up and pulled him onto her lap.

So lost in the scene was Katie that she had no idea how long she had been standing there when Alexandria, as if sensing her presence, gently lifted the young child out of her lap and turned around. Katie pulled open the door, but didn't enter.

"It's Andrew's turn now," Alexandria said quietly. "I want you to surf the 'Net until you can tell me how many stars there are in the galaxy, okay?"

The young man nodded.

"I need to go now," Alexandria explained, "but I'll be back soon."

"Oh, Alex, can't you stay?" the young man said as he grabbed her around the neck. Alexandria didn't flinch, but gently removed the child's arms.

"Next time, Andrew," she said touching the young child on his cheek. "And Dr. Davis says it's time for you to start your treatments."

The young man frowned. "I don't want to," he said.

"I know," Alexandria said glancing back at Katie, "but you have to. That's just the way it is. Remember what I told you." The young boy looked solemnly at her as she said, "You're all strong enough on the inside to get your shots and treatments when you need to. You'll be strong on the outside once they're over with. I'll see you all soon."

"Bye, Alex," they all shouted.

ALEXANDRIA STOOD UP AND without saying a word, walked out the doors past Katie. Katie could barely keep up with her and practically had to pry the elevator doors back open before they slammed shut in her face.

"Alex, please," she said. "I'm sorry. I had no idea," she blurted out.

Alexandria stared silently at the numbers on the elevator as they counted down. Right before the doors opened, Alex asked, "Who else knows?"

"Just me and Antoine, unless he mentioned it to Marcus."

When they reached the lobby of the hospital, Katie ran ahead of her and cut her off.

"Alex, wait."

Alexandria glanced away.

"I needed to find you," Katie explained. "My mother, Linda Jordan, and their friend, Mr. Collins were kidnapped from Shamrock Shores a few hours ago. My mother sent an e-mail on behalf of Linda Jordan, and I need you to analyze her computer and find out what it said."

"Fine," Alex said as she headed toward the street.

All the warmth Katie had witnessed just a few minutes ago evaporated into the air like the morning mist. Back in place was the steely reserve Katie was so familiar with.

They all assembled in the conference room.

"How's the search on the e-mail going?" Katie asked.

"Sorting it as we speak," Alexandria said as she suddenly reached into her pocket and pulled out her vibrating cell phone.

"Please," Katie begged. "I need you here now."

Alexandria silenced the phone, and returned it to her pocket. Within seconds, e-mails appeared on-screen.

"There, that one. The one addressed to carly@ryanandrogers. com."

Dear Miss Ryan:
    Our mutual friend, Linda Jordan, has been staying with me to complete the revisions. She asked me to let you know that the project is complete and she will be delivering it to you in person tomorrow, as previously agreed. When and where would you like to meet?
    Sincerely,
    Molly Mahoney

"Crap, she gave her full name."

"I don't understand. How could whoever this person is, know where Molly was just by an e-mail?" Jane asked.

"Whoever is behind this obviously is able to monitor all e-mail traffic. Additionally, it wouldn't take much to sort through on-line public records to see the purchase agreement for her place at Shamrock Shores. Did she get a reply back?" Katie asked as she paced back and forth.

"Here it is."

```
Dear Ms. Mahoney:
    Thank you for relaying the message. Can
you please advise Linda that we will meet
her at The Coastal at two p.m. on Friday and
we're all very excited to receive her new
package.
    Best regards,
    Carly Ryan
```

"Do you see anything else?"

"There is one thing…"

"What's that?"

"Someone at your mom's place has been visiting some interesting sites on their community computer. Sorry Jane," Alexandria said as a picture appeared on screen of a young naked woman named "Dolly Llama," whose breasts far outweighed her beauty.

"Dolly Llama, my ass," Margo began. "Don't even try to tell me those twins are real. One good poke with a sharp object and she'd be flying and buzzing all around the room."

"Frankly, darlings, I don't see why you girls feel the need to inflate your tires so," Marcus said. "The only thing I want to see pumped up is…"

"Marcus!" Margo yelled.

"I agree with Marcus. It seems such a shame that young women cannot accept their bodies the way God intended them to be," Jane began. "Such poor self-image."

"She can't be that poor. I bet you those silicone Sallies cost a pretty penny," Margo said. Hoisting her own assets in the air, she said, "Fortunately, I've been naturally blessed in that department."

Katie walked up to the screen and stared at the picture of the girl.

"If you'd like to meet her, Katarina, darling, I'm sure that can be arranged," Marcus said.

Margo swatted at her brother, nearly causing him to spill his drink, but Katie remained standing in front of the screen, transfixed.

"Katie?" Margo finally asked.

Katie whipped around. "Alex, bring up the video I took the other day when Linda Jordan went for her swim."

The camera panned *The Two of Us* as the man and woman made preparations to leave the slip.

"Another over-inflated job," Margo said as she watched the amply endowed woman in the hot pink bikini.

Katie walked over to a table, picked up a folder and flipped through it.

"What's the matter?" Jane asked.

"According to our notes, the wife said the TOW has worked for years as a waitress in a chain restaurant."

"So?"

"So how is it that a waitress is able to afford her bump-out additions?"

"Maybe she saved up? Up and out, I mean," Margo added.

"I once considered an enlargement," Marcus said as he dipped his finger in his drink and licked it, "but Captain Antoine assured me it wasn't necessary."

"Thanks for that," Katie said sarcastically. "Did we ever run these people? Ever do a background?"

"No," Margo said, "we thought we were looking at an open and shut case of a philandering husband and his TOW WOMB."

"TOW WOMB?" Antoine asked.

"The Other Woman, Woman of Mighty Breasts," Margo explained.

"Let's reopen it," Katie said. "Let's start by running the marine registration for *The Two of Us.*"

"You're going to reopen a case based on the fact that a waitress has big balloons?" Margo asked.

"No. I'm reopening it because of this." Turning to Alexandria, she said, "Rewind the video from the beginning and keep it going."

Katie pointed to the big screen. They all watched as the man stood at the helm and repeatedly glanced across several times.

"Do you see that?" she asked.

"See what? That he keeps looking up and over?"

"Yes."

"You think we were spotted?"

"No."

"Then who the hell is he looking at …," Margo said as she realized exactly what Katie was thinking.

"I don't understand," Jane said. "What is it?"

"He's not looking at *The FlameBoyant*," Katie explained.

"Then who is he looking at?"

"There was only one other person at the docks that morning," Katie said.

"You think these people may somehow be tied to your mother and Linda Jordan being kidnapped?" Jane asked.

"It's the only thing we have to go on right now."

MARCUS PICKED UP HIS drink, grabbed Antoine by the arm, and steered him toward the door.

"Let's go, my Adonis, I have a feeling the black widows will soon be spinning their silvery webs and we don't want to get caught in them. In the meantime, let's make absolutely certain about that enlargement. Good luck finding your friends, darlings…"

KATIE GRABBED THE CASE folder and began flipping through it. "Tom Langevin, age forty-eight. Executive VP with …" she paused and glanced at Alexandria, "TBI Pharmaceuticals."

Alexandria looked up for a second, then went back to the laptop.

"Bring up the State's database of marine registrations," Katie said.

Katie watched on the big screen as *The Two of Us* came back to "TBI Pharmaceuticals."

"Alex?"

Alexandria stopped typing.

"Can I see you in the Cybercision Center for a minute please?"

"Alright, what the hell is going on?" Katie asked as she paced back and forth in front of the bank of computers.

"What do you mean?"

"I don't have time for games, Alex. I walked in here the other day and you had a number of screens on search engines with TBI Pharmaceuticals as the subject."

Alexandria walked over to Divinity's cage and picked her up in the palm of her hand and began to slowly stroke her.

"So?"

"I want to know what the hell is going on!" Katie yelled. "It was the cell phone, wasn't it? You traced the cell phone back to them."

"I can't tell you."

"Alex, do you understand that three lives may depend on it?"

Alexandria spun around. "Do you understand that tens of thousands of lives may depend on my not telling you?"

"What?"

Alexandria set Divinity back down in her cage and reached for a live cricket which she placed in the corner of the glass aquarium. Divinity crouched, sensing her dinner nearby.

"Do you remember that young boy, Andrew, I was with a little while ago?"

Katie recalled the young man sitting, unbelievably, in Alexandria's lap.

"Yes."

"He's undergoing a highly experimental treatment with a radical new manufactured drug."

"And?"

"And that drug is manufactured by TBI Pharmaceuticals."

Katie shook her head. "So?"

"Katie, Linda Jordan's sequel is all about the lack of federal oversight on experimental drug treatments, especially for cancer patients."

Given Alexandria's background, Katie knew enough not to ask how she knew that.

"She's got enough clout now that if she releases the book, there's a strong probability that companies like TBI Pharmaceuticals will come under scrutiny and possibly have their operations suspended." Alexandria shook her head. "It's working, Katie. The drug is working."

"And you think TBI Pharmaceuticals is behind all of this…"

Alexandria didn't answer.

"Alex, look, I'm sorry. If the drug works, it works, but my mother's life is at stake here."

"I know."

"Please, Alex. You've got to help me. Where can I find them?"

"They have offices at the tradeport."

16

THE SUN WAS BEGINNING to set as Katie and Alexandria arrived at the former airport, now a burgeoning industrial park and trade-port. A few small commercial airlines still used the runway. Silver planes glistened in the setting sun. Most of the businesses were already closed with few cars in the parking lots.

Katie slowly circled the offices of TBI Pharmaceuticals. Not seeing anyone, she turned the corner and spotted a dark green sedan parked near a flat, unmarked warehouse.

The warehouse had a large freight door and a smaller regular-sized door as well as some small windows set very high, too high for Katie or Alexandria to be able to see into without a ladder. Katie slowed the van down to a crawl and pulled in far enough away not to be heard or seen.

Instinctively, she pulled her jacket aside and withdrew her weapon to check the gun's safety.

"Do you think you'll need that?" Alex asked.

"As Ma always says, better to have it and not need it, than need it and not have it," Katie said, as she surveyed the area. "Other than the freight door, there's only one door in, and we have to assume it may be locked. I wish we could see inside."

"We can, there's a utility pole on the side."

"So?"

"I could shimmy up the pole and onto the roof if you wanted."

"And then what?"

"We still have the pinhole cameras from the Levine case in the back of the van."

KATIE WATCHED WITH AMAZEMENT as Alexandria easily shimmied up the utility pole using her hands and bare feet to hoist her thin body up and onto the roof. In her black outfit, she truly resembled a human spider. Using a wireless headset, she whispered back down to Katie.

"There are dead things up here."

"Ignore them. Like my father always used to say: if they're dead, they can't hurt you."

Alexandria carefully stretched over the edge and using a thin network cable as a tether, lowered the camera. Katie hopped into the back of the van and brought up the display.

"One bad guy dressed in black," she relayed. "I suspect this is our boat driver as well. He's got them all tied up. They're sitting next to each other on crates just underneath you. They're all moving and alive," she said with much relief.

"I think I can hear voices," Alexandria said.

"Now might be a good time to approach if we can do it quickly and quietly."

"I'll be right down."

Alexandria quickly shimmied back down the pole, slipped her shoes back on and met Katie at the door to the warehouse. Katie turned the knob, but it was locked.

"Now what?" Alexandria whispered.

Putting her fingers to her lips, Katie reached into her pocket and took out a small black pouch. Flipping it open, she revealed what appeared to be a bunch of tiny saws and blades. Working quickly, Katie slipped several picks into the door until she heard a small "click."

"Low tech," she whispered.

She carefully placed the tools back into her blazer pocket and nodded to Alexandria. Pushing Alexandria behind her and away from the door frame, she placed her hand on the butt of her gun, withdrew it and turned the knob. She and Alexandria slipped through. Alexandria almost let the door slam shut, but Katie caught it at the last second and very slowly leaned it closed.

Katie's mother, Linda Jordan, and Timothy Collins were seated on crates at the far end of the warehouse. Linda Jordan was no longer wearing the silver fob around her neck. Their hands were all bound behind them with rope. Her mother's knitting bag rested on the floor beside her. A man dressed in black jeans and a black

T-shirt with a silver handgun tucked into his waist stood nearby studying his nails as if he were bored to tears.

There was quite a distance and many crates stamped TBI Pharmaceuticals between them. Crouching down and keeping their heads low, Katie and Alexandria slowly began to weave through the maze of crates toward them.

"Excuse me, young man, I wonder if I might bother you for a moment?" Katie heard her mother ask.

"What?"

"This whole thing seems awfully silly," her mother reasoned. "We're harmless senior citizens. No offense, Linda."

"None taken and I'd rather think of it as the golden years."

"What's that?" Timothy Collins said.

"She said, 'think of it as the golden years,'" Molly Mahoney repeated quite loudly.

"He's got gold in here?" Timothy Collins replied as he scanned around the room.

"Look, Lady, why don't you sit there and keep quiet."

"You got what you want, didn't you? Can't you just let us go?"

"No."

"What harm could we possibly bring to you?" Molly implored.

Katie and Alexandria took turns maneuvering between the crates as Katie signaled to Alex whenever it was safe to move forward. The distance between the parties began to close up.

"Excuse me, young man," Katie's mother asked a moment later.

"What now?"

"I have a small problem," she said coyly. "And I'm afraid it can't wait much longer. I need to use the facilities. I have … incontinent issues."

"What's that?" Timothy Collins asked.

"I said I have incontinent issues," Molly repeated louder.

"Who's incompetent!" screamed Timothy Collins. "Is that what he just called you? Why you little …"

"Oh, for heavens sake, Timothy!" Molly Mahoney shouted, "Why didn't you wear your aids today?"

"They'll be a raid alright!" he shouted back.

"Really, he's not this bad when he wears them," Molly assured Linda Jordan.

"Please! All of you shut up!" the man yelled.

"May the Good Lord forgive you for putting us in harm's way," her mother said resolutely.

"Lady," the young man said withdrawing the gun from his waist, "if you don't shut up, one of your friends here will be dying first."

"Who's dying of thirst?" Timothy Collins asked. "I went for seven days straight without food or water during the war."

"Just shut up!" the man screamed. Even Timothy Collins heard him that time. They all grew silent as the man's cell phone began to ring.

"Hello? Yeah, I've got it, Boss," Katie heard him say as he reached into his pocket, withdrew the silver fob and flipped it around on the chain. He was too busy waving it to see Katie inching forward.

"What do you want me to do with them?" he asked. Katie saw his eyes narrow. "Are you sure, Boss? But they're all witnesses. If you say so. Yeah, she was wearing it when I grabbed her. Okay, I'll see you in a few," he said as he closed the phone and slipped the fob back into his pocket.

The man tucked the gun back into his waistband and walked toward them.

"Stand up," he ordered.

"Hail Mary, full of Grace ..." Katie heard her mother begin to say.

"Shut up!" the man shouted. "On your feet. We're going for a ride."

Katie and Alexandria, still hidden by the crates, moved silently behind him. Using her hands to signal, she gestured to Alexandria to take care of the three as she went around the other side of the crate to surprise the man. She silently drew her weapon from its holster, but did not release the safety just yet.

Katie stood up. Her mother gave a loud gasp and the man turned on his heels to see why. Alexandria jumped behind Katie's mother and quickly began to undo the knots as the man reached for the gun in his waistband. In a split second, Katie released the safety on the weapon, placed her finger on the trigger, and faced him.

"Freeze!" she shouted. "Don't even think about it. Get your hands up. Now!"

"Heaven have mercy, it's Katie!" her mother yelled. "I told you it would be alright, Linda," she said as Alexandria freed her hands and began to work on Linda Jordan's restraints.

"Stay there, Ma," Katie called, but it was too late. Her mother, clutching her knitting bag, came running toward her, placing herself between Katie and the young man. Katie winced and had no choice but to lift her weapon to avoid putting her mother in the line of fire. The young man caught the movement, withdrew his weapon from his waistband, grabbed Molly Mahoney by the arm as she passed by, and yanked her back. Using Molly as a shield, he put the gun to her head.

"One move and she dies."

"Jesus, Mary, and Joseph," Katie heard her mother say quietly.

"Drop the gun or she gets it!" he yelled. Katie put the safety back on and slowly bent down toward the floor. She looked at her mother's face and saw the fear in her eyes.

"It's okay, Ma. Just listen to me. It will be okay."

Her mother gave her a small nod.

Knowing she had no choice, Katie reluctantly set her gun down on the floor of the warehouse.

"Kick it toward me," the young man ordered. Katie was careful not to actually kick the gun for fear of an accidental discharge, but gave it a small nudge. The young man picked up her gun and tucked it into his back pocket.

"All of you, get over there," he said gesturing with the barrel of the gun to where Alexandria and Linda stood motionless, unsure of what to do. Timothy Collins was still tied up.

"Why you lousy...," Timothy muttered. "If you harm any of these ladies...," he said, shaking his head.

"You won't get away with this," Katie said. "What do you think you're going to do, kill five innocent people? They'll throw you in the gas chamber in a second. Besides, the police are already on their way."

"Really? You'd better hope they're not or this one," he said, yanking Molly by the arm, "gets it first. Now shut up and get over there with the others."

Katie was loath to put distance between she and her mother. Feeling she was only safe if she could somehow find an opportunity to take him down, she kept talking.

"What makes you think that's the only copy?" Katie asked.

The man squinted his eyes. "I know it is."

"Think about it, you think she'd be crazy enough to keep just one copy?"

"She's been quoted all over the place, saying that she only keeps one copy."

"She made forty million from *The Franklin Cure*. You think she'd risk another forty million dollars by not having backup copies? Does that make any sense to you?"

Out of the corner of her eye, Katie noticed her mother's left hand slip down into her knitting bag that was resting by her side.

"I'll pay you three million to let everyone walk out of here safely," Linda Jordan announced. "You wouldn't have to share it with anyone."

The mere idea of anyone being able to arbitrarily come up with three million dollars hung in the air between them for several seconds.

"Imagine what you could do with three million dollars all your own," Katie said, as she tried not to waste time pondering the idea for herself. She could tell she had him thinking. He shifted his stance slightly and cocked his head to the side. Katie glanced at her mother and gave a tiny nod.

Molly Mahoney, in one quick motion, withdrew a long knitting needle and without even glancing at its intended direction, forcefully stuck the young man with it.

HE IMMEDIATELY DOUBLED UP and clutched at his groin, loosening his grip just enough for Molly to slip away from him. Katie lunged forward and tried to grab at her own gun that was in his back pocket, but it slipped and fell to the floor. Focusing her entire body on the gun he still held in his hand, she tried to jam the piece of skin between her thumb and pointer finger in between the firing mechanism. The two went flying against the wall of the warehouse. Somewhere in the midst of the struggle, she heard Timothy Collins yell, "Untie me now!"

"Help me get him untied," she heard her mother call as they all ran to Timothy Collins' chair.

Katie prayed that the gun didn't discharge inside the warehouse, knowing that in such tight quarters, even if by some miracle no one was hit by a ricocheting bullet, the sound of the discharge alone could cause deafness. She wrapped her other hand around his gun hand and dug her nails deep into his flesh as he grabbed at her neck with his free hand, squeezing with all his might.

Recalling her days of hand-to-hand defensive training, Katie lowered her neck as tight as she could against his grip. Suddenly, she felt another body next to hers but didn't dare lift her head to see who it was. It was with some shock that she recognized the long, pale fingers and black nail polish as Alexandria tried desperately to pry the young man's hands off Katie's neck.

Katie kept her focus entirely on the gun. It was a short-barreled Smith & Wesson thirty-eight special. She looked at the gun and saw blood, unsure whose it was. The young man kept a tight squeeze on Katie's neck, despite Alexandria digging her fingernails deep into his hand as she tried to pry his fingers back.

"Let her go, now!" she heard Timothy Collins shout just as she heard the familiar sound of a magazine being racked. The young man heard it too, and temporarily loosened his grip enough to turn and see Timothy Collins pointing Katie's gun directly at his head in a perfect stance.

"Do it! Now!" Timothy Collins shouted.

The young man loosened his grip. Katie clutched one hand to her throat as she gasped for breath. Regaining her strength, she pried the gun out of his hand. As soon as she had his weapon secured, the young man pitched forward and clutched at his groin. Katie turned to see Linda and her mother standing next to Timothy Collins, knitting needles poised and at the ready.

Katie handed the young man's revolver over to Timothy Collins and observed his excellent shooting stance—elbows slightly angled, fingers loose on the grip of the weapon, trigger finger alongside the trigger, poised and ready to fire. Without even looking down, Timothy Collins instinctively tucked the weapon into his waistband.

"Cover me, Mr. Collins," Katie shouted as she withdrew the handcuffs from her waist.

"What's that?" Timothy Collins asked.

"I said, cover me!" Katie shouted.

"Right-o."

KATIE WALKED BEHIND THE young man, who was still clutching at his groin, and slipped her handcuffs on him.

"You were right, by the way," she said as she dug into his pocket and handed the silver fob back to Linda Jordan, "it is the only copy."

THE YOUNG MAN SAT in the back of the "Divinity Florals" van as his eyes swept around at all of the electronic equipment and monitors. His cell phone began to ring.

"I'll remind you of the charges, Kevin," Katie said before he opened it up. "Three counts of kidnapping, five counts of criminal threatening, one count of aggravated assault..."

"I know, I know," he said. Katie nodded. The small cable Alexandria had attached to his phone fed into one of their computers. "Hello? Yeah, I've still got it. No, I just got tied up a little. That's all. Where are you? Okay, I'll be right over."

He hung up as Katie took the cell phone from him, unplugged it and placed it in her own pocket.

"Did you get it?" Katie asked Alexandria.

"The call came from the beach. Ocean and Seaview. I trapped the incoming number as well."

Katie glanced out the window. "Let's go," she said as she grabbed the man under the arm. He winced as he stepped down out of the van. Katie led him back to the warehouse, and with the help of Timothy Collins and Alexandria, shoved him inside one of the crates marked "TBI Pharmaceuticals," before securing the lid with a chain and padlock from the van. They wedged a block of wood in the cover to make sure he had enough air.

"You can't!" he yelled. "I'll suffocate and die. Please!" he begged.

"No, you won't," Katie assured him. "You've got plenty of air and we'll send someone for you as soon as we're done with our business."

"Please," he screamed. "Please don't leave me here. I've told you everything."

"You should have thought of that before you put these women in harm's way," Timothy Collins said as he double-checked that the lock was secure. "That'll teach him." Turning to Katie, he said, "Are you sure you don't want me to stand guard?"

"No, Mr. Collins, but I do need you to make a few other deliveries," Katie said.

"Eateries? Who could eat at a time like this?"

"You're sure you're okay, Ma?" Katie asked as she placed a kiss on her mother's cheek. Molly Mahoney was seated next to Timothy Collins, who drove the young man's car. Linda Jordan was slunk down low in the back seat.

"Other than needing something to steady my nerves, I'll be fine. Are you alright, dear?" she asked, touching Katie's neck.

"I'm fine, Ma. Can't keep a good woman down."

"It was terribly frightening, but exciting at the same time. Don't you think so, Linda?"

"Honestly, I think I've had enough excitement for today, Molly."

Katie went around to the driver's side.

"I want to thank you, Mr. Collins. As far as I'm concerned you saved my life," she said, patting him on the arm.

"Thanks for asking, but she passed away six years ago."

KATIE WATCHED THEM DRIVE off. Glancing at her watch, she realized they had less than twenty-four hours to deliver the manuscript.

"Let's go," she said as she climbed back in the van next to Alexandria.

"What now?"

Katie reached into her pocket and took out the phony silver fob that Jane had worn during the library dedication. "Let's see what sharks we can entice with our pretty silver lure ..."

Alexandria kept her hands on her lap. "Katie, now that your mom and everyone else are safe, couldn't we just let things go ..."

"Until that manuscript is delivered," Katie reminded her, "no one is safe. Come on."

Alexandria reluctantly started the ignition just as Katie's cell phone began to ring.

"Hello. Hey, Kel," she said to her sister—and almost immediately pulled the phone away from her ear. Alexandria could hear Katie's sister's raised voice from the driver's side.

"Cool it, Kel, she's fine. They're all fine. I didn't tell you because no one was supposed to know. She'll be back at Shamrock Shores in just a few minutes. I didn't tell you because I wasn't sure what was going on. She'll be a regular celebrity. Do her good to have a little excitement once in her life. No, I'm not being facetious. Look, would you please calm down? You know what, Kel? I'm beginning to wonder if you're really upset because Ma had a little trouble or because you're the last to know that she was roommates with Linda Jordan. Well, that's what it sounds like to me. Would you please calm down? I didn't put her in harm's way," Katie lied. "She's fine. A little tired, but fine." Katie scratched the front of the mouthpiece. "Sorry, but I'm losing a signal now. I'll call you later," she said as she abruptly snapped the cell phone shut and shoved it back in her pocket.

KATIE SAT IN THE van and skimmed the crowd. It wasn't hard to spot Tom Langevin. He was sitting with his WOMB at an outdoor café sipping a glass of wine. The woman was dressed in a tight pink sweater over a pair of very short shorts. Katie thought if yarn had feelings, it would be crying from being stretched out so far. Katie saw Tom Langevin glance anxiously at his watch several times before reaching for his cell phone.

"Hello?"

"Why, hello, Tom."

"Who is this?"

"Let's just say I'm the person who has the item that you want."

"Where's Kevin?"

"Kevin had to go away for a little while. He left something behind, which I'm willing to negotiate with you about."

"Negotiate?"

"Send your over-inflated girlfriend for a hike, and we'll talk." She could see Tom Langevin glance around anxiously as he leaned forward and said something to the young woman, who promptly got up, gave him a dismissive look, and strutted away.

"See that white van with the flowers on the side of it parked near the hot dog stand?"

"Yes."

"Walk toward it."

Katie kept her weapon holstered beneath her blazer and jumped out to meet Tom Langevin. He was in his mid-fifties, a nice-looking man, wearing an open-collared sports shirt and khakis. He had the ease of a man who was used to comforts. Katie peered at him over her sunglasses.

"Who are you?" he asked.

"Who I am doesn't matter," Katie began. "Just walk with me," she said as she turned toward the beach.

"How do I even know you have what I'm interested in?" he asked.

Katie reached into her jacket pocket and dangled the silver fob in front of him before quickly tucking it away again.

"Where did you get that?"

"From Kevin. Let's just say his balls got all knotted up."

"He didn't ... Dear God, I never meant for ..."

Katie stopped. "What? You didn't want your company to be facing murder charges?"

"Oh, dear God," Tom Langevin said as Katie watched the blood drain from his face. "I specifically told him not to hurt anyone. I'm a retired medical doctor. I swear to you, I never meant for anyone to get hurt. If he said otherwise, he's lying."

"I would be able to believe you a lot better if it weren't for the fact that Linda Jordan almost got killed the other day, and you were just a few waves away."

"What are you talking about?"

"The other morning on the water. Linda Jordan's boat was overturned by some idiot in a cigarette boat who decided to send her into the ocean for a swim."

"Is that what happened?" he asked, so sincerely that Katie almost believed him. "Vanessa and I … that's my friend … Vanessa and I were down below. We were … occupied. I wondered what caused that wake."

"Do you honestly expect me to believe that you had nothing to do with it? You were there."

"I'm telling you, whoever you are, that I didn't have anything to do with it."

"And you didn't know it was Linda Jordan on that boat?"

She saw the pause in his step.

"I thought I recognized her. I had heard from the marina owner that she had a boat moored there. Then I saw the name on the boat and put two and two together, but I swear to you, I never meant for her or anyone else to get hurt."

Katie watched some young children kicking a beach ball around.

"Look," Tom Langevin began again, "I've admitted everything to you so far. I only wanted to try and get the copy of the book

153

because of all the damage it could do to my company, but I never intended to hurt anyone. That's the truth..."

"So you offered a two-million-dollar bounty for it."

"Not just my company. There's an entire conglomerate of pharmaceutical companies that put up the money. No one wanted to see the book published once we heard what it was about."

"The book will be published, either way," Katie announced. "Your company is going to have to weather the storm along with everyone else. If you get scrutinized because of the publicity, so be it. That can't be stopped."

Tom Langevin stopped and looked across at the ocean and shook his head.

"No one was supposed to get hurt."

"No one has."

"What?" he said as he turned back. "But you said..."

"So far, no one has been hurt."

The look of relief that crossed his face was legitimate.

"You said you would be willing to negotiate. Negotiate what?"

Katie twisted her mouth and faced him.

"As much as I'd love to see you go down because of your involvement, I actually believe you and, from what I'm told, the drug your company manufactures may be saving lives."

"Of course it's saving lives. We're in the business of saving lives."

"So here's the deal. I'm willing to overlook your company's involvement in this little debacle if you promise me that you and your goons won't make any more foolish attempts to go after Linda Jordan or the manuscript. I'm holding you personally responsible for calling off the others as well."

"That's it?"

"For now, yes. Oh, and by the way, I suggest you send someone over to your warehouse at the tradeport to take care of a package left behind there," she said as she strolled off, leaving Tom Langevin in a mixed state of both relief and confusion.

It was late afternoon before Katie and Alexandria returned to the offices of the Black Widow Agency. Linda Jordan, having been safely delivered back by Timothy Collins, sat in the conference room chair across from Marcus. They both had a pinkish drink in their hands.

"I just spoke with my mother," Katie began. "Word has spread rapidly that she was, emphasis on was, harboring a famous guest, and rumors are that she was kidnapped by a gang. She and Mr. Collins are enjoying their temporary celebrity status. If I know my mother, and I do, there's bound to be quite a party there tonight."

"I'm so glad she's alright, Katie. I'm glad we're all alright," Linda said as she raised her glass. "Here's to everyone being safe and sound."

Marcus flashed his brown eyes at her and raised his glass.

"What have you got there?" Katie asked eyeing Linda's glass.

"I'm not sure. Marcus made it for me. It's apple juice, Grenadine, lemon juice, and vodka. Is that right?"

"Perfect, Miss Linda. You're a good student."

"Did you ask him what it was called?" Katie said to Linda.

"No."

"Good. You don't ever want to ask Marcus what his drinks are called."

Linda thought about this for a moment, but curiosity got the better of her. "Marcus?" she asked as she held the drink up to the light.

"It's called 'Bare Cheeks,' in honor of my beloved," he said as he pursed his lips at Antoine.

"You had to ask," Katie said. "In the meantime, we need to find a place to keep you safe for the night and right now, I'm thinking that this may be the best place, but I'll need everyone's help. We'll need to take turns being on watch. Margo, I know you need to be home to take care of Trevor, so you're excused from this duty."

"I'm sure my mom can watch him for the night," Margo said. "I'll give her a call."

"Yes, Mother loves to spoil that child," Marcus piped in.

"Because he's the son she never had."

"True," Marcus said.

"At least she doesn't catch him sneaking around, trying on her underwear."

"I thought a pushup would enhance my figure," Marcus said as he sipped his drink.

Katie stifled a yawn. "We're all going to have to take turns. Two to a shift. Margo and Alex, you'll take the first shift. Marcus and Antoine can take the second, and Jane and I will take the third. That way everyone gets some sleep. We'll crash right in here. It will be like a big campout."

"Hold your testosterone," Marcus interrupted. "How did we get volunteered for this duty? Perhaps my beloved and I had other plans *c'est soir.*"

"We didn't, Marcus," Antoine said. "Besides, you always told me how much you loved campouts."

"Yes, when they were filled with other boys and doubled-up sleeping bags. Do you see any of that here, excusing Katarina, of course."

Margo swatted him on the arm.

"You know I could take you if I wanted to, Marcus," Katie said putting her hands on her hips. "It's a good thing I'm tired. Now can I count on the two of you or not?"

"Of course you can," Antoine said, patting his partner on the leg. "You can always count on us. Right, Marcus?"

"I'm thinking about it," Marcus said as he swirled his pink drink around.

"Marcus," his sister said, "if you do this, I'll make s'mores for you."

"In that case, you can definitely count us in."

"Thank you," Katie said. "Now that that's settled, we need to focus on a plan to deliver the manuscript."

"THAT LOOKS WONDERFUL," LINDA Jordan said a little while later, as Margo distributed the plates. "What is it?"

"Peppered tuna steaks with cilantro and basil and dilled potato salad," Margo replied. "Just something I whipped up."

"We're very fortunate, as you can see," Katie explained, "to have Margo on our team."

"I'll say," Linda said, as she bit in. Antoine did the honors of opening a bottle of Chardonnay.

"One glass each," Katie announced. "I need everyone on their toes."

"Speak for yourself, Katarina. If you're going to force us into babysitting, the least you can do is make the atmosphere pleasant," Marcus whined.

"I mean it, Marcus, I need everyone alert."

ALEX SIPPED A DIET soda and barely touched her food. Margo rolled her eyes at her. "Now if Momma was here," Margo said holding her fork in the air, "she'd set your skinny little white ass in that chair and make you stay until you had eaten everything up. Which, of course," Margo said swaying her ample hips, "is how I got all these bulges."

"The only bulges I'm interested in...," Marcus began to say but Margo, who was seated next to her brother, took her fork and stabbed him in the arm with it.

"Ow!" he yelled.

"Serves you damn right."

"If you don't mind," Linda said observing them in action, "I'm just curious about something... Have the two of you always been so... contentious? Aren't twins supposed to be especially compatible?"

"He's been competing with me over everything since the day he slipped out of that damn canal," Margo explained. "Barbies, Easy Bake Ovens, high heels, boyfriends... especially boyfriends.

It's always been each man for himself, or in our case, each woman for herself."

"I'm not the one who couldn't tell that Tyrone Withers was more homo than sapien," Marcus said as he nibbled on a piece of tuna. "But let me assure you by the time I was done with that boy, he was upright."

"Okay," Katie said interrupting and snapping her fingers. "I think Linda gets the point. In the meantime, we still need to come up with a way to get that," she said pointing to the silver fob around Linda's neck, "to Ryan & Rogers."

Linda picked up the fob and rubbed it.

"I keep thinking, Miss Linda," Marcus began, "that one of these times you'll rub that little pendant of yours and a genie will appear. Of course, if it could be *I Dream of Jeannie* that would be divine. That girl knew fashion. Those lovely gauchos accompanied with a splash of shimmering rhinestone. Do you remember when Jeannie's evil cousin pretended to be her and poor Tony could never tell the difference? Of course if my beloved Antoine ever had a double, I'd know in an instant which was the real thing by the size of his ..."

"Wait a minute," Katie said, interrupting. "That's it. That's how we can pull this off."

"Gauchos and rhinestones?" Marcus asked. "Or the size of something very special? Do count me in."

"No, but if they can't tell the difference between the real Linda Jordan and the pretend Linda Jordan ..."

Jane dropped her fork on her plate. "Oh, Katie, please. You promised me I'd never have to be Linda again. Oh dear, that didn't sound very nice. Forgive me," Jane said as she fanned herself with her napkin, "I didn't mean it that way."

"Of course not," Linda said. "No offense taken."

"Just one more time, Janie, it's really the only way. I swear this will be the last. I just need you to be a decoy. I don't expect anything will happen at all, but just in case…"

LATER ON, THEY ALL huddled down on the carpet on blankets and throw pillows of chenille and tapestry from Marcus and Antoine's stockroom. Everyone, even Alexandria, devoured the s'mores that Margo made. Alexandria brought up a website displaying a virtual campfire, including the sound of crackling logs, on the big screen.

"If anyone starts singing any damn camp songs, I'll whoop their ass," Margo announced.

"You mean like 'Homo, Homo on the Range'?" her brother asked. "One of my personal favorites." Antoine laughed.

"You start singing that and I'm gonna show you what a 'Broke Back' is really all about. You got me, Brother?"

"Heavens to Barbra Streisand," Marcus said, tsking away.

"This is kind of nice," Katie said sitting cross-legged on the floor, leaning against a couch and looking at the fire. "Maybe we should do this on a regular basis."

"Oddly enough, I have a campfire to thank for my writing career," Linda Jordan said.

"Really? How so?"

"I grew up west of here, near Noack Mountain. My parents cherished that mountain, loved the outdoors, and built campfires for the family all the time. My mother would sit my brothers and sister and I around the campfire while she regaled us with stories. Sometimes they would be light and fanciful and we would know right away that it was a creation of her mind. After all, not many women actually have twenty-two children, all with bright red hair, living in one room, or are descended from fairies with magical powers that allow people to fly, but other times she'd tell us real stories of great heroes or scientists. Occasionally, she'd tell a scary story that would send chills up our spine, but each time after she told us a story, she'd pick up a warm stone from the base of the campfire and pass it around. When the stone came to you, it was your turn to tell a story. It didn't matter how long or short it was, or how true or untrue it was. What mattered was that you shared. It planted the seeds of imagination and creativity that grew and grew over a lifetime. I cherished my turn to tell my stories as much as I cherished listening to her tell hers. And so it all began."

"And a lovely story that was," Jane offered. "It seems the skills of storytelling have been largely lost from our culture."

"While I agree that culturally we've lost the art of passing stories from generation to generation, I'd like to think that stories are still being passed down in every book that gets published. That's why I work so hard to make my books entertaining."

"They're entertaining, alright," Alexandria said quietly.

Linda Jordan did not miss the tone of sarcasm in her voice. "Alexandria," she said gently, "I have had the strong sense since we first met that you somehow disapprove of what I do."

Katie quickly jumped in. "Alex can be funny sometimes," she tried to say. "It's just the way she is."

Alexandria stared at Katie for a few seconds, then turned to Linda Jordan. "It's dangerous to write about something you know so little about."

"But I did extensive research for *The Franklin Cure*. I consulted with some of the top experts in the medical field. In fact," she said glancing around as she took them into her confidence, "few people realize this, but there actually was a document that prescribed almost the same formula I quoted in the book. I made little note of it publicly for fear it would just fuel the controversy further."

"And yet you were willing to allow patients, desperate patients with little hope, to take the risk of trying what was really an archaic formula based on nineteenth-century knowledge and extremely dangerous practices instead of embracing modern technology and contemporary medical techniques that have been proven to work."

Everyone sat in stunned silence. Linda Jordan narrowed her eyes and stared quizzically at Alexandria.

"I sense this is personal for you."

Alexandria glanced momentarily toward Antoine and then put her head down. "Yes."

"I'm sorry. As I've said over and over, it is a work of fiction."

"A work of fiction that was so popular that the AMA had to take out a full page ad in leading newspapers and magazines begging patients to stop trying the formula and heed their doctor's advice. You don't find that irresponsible?"

Katie cleared her throat. "It's late," she said. "Maybe we should all try and get some sleep now."

"Since the book was released," Linda Jordan began, ignoring Katie, "more than ten million dollars has been raised toward cancer research in its name. Medical scholars are poring over all of the research to see what has worked and what hasn't. I have personally donated ten percent of the profits, that's four million dollars, to several charities promoting cancer research and to provide housing for cancer patients and their families while they undergo treatment. Since the book was released, annual screenings and mammograms have risen eighteen percent. Since the book was released, the First Lady allowed the media to follow her until she entered the room for her annual mammogram. The Surgeon General, herself, was quoted as saying she believed no other book in the history of publishing has drawn so much attention to cancer awareness."

Awkwardness fell upon the room as they looked at each other. "I am truly sorry for whatever you or your loved ones have suffered, but I have to believe that the book has raised both an awareness and consciousness that did not exist prior to its publication. It is a story, however, and I am a storyteller. I will not wallow in guilt for those who cannot distinguish fact from fiction."

"Then you obviously don't know what it's like to be desperate."

Turning to Margo, Alex said, "It's our shift. If you don't mind, I'll watch from the Cybercision Center to make sure no one approaches the building." She got up and walked out.

"Did Mr. Spock just have a damn breakdown or something?" Margo asked.

"I'm sorry," Katie said to Linda Jordan. "She … it's complicated."

Linda nodded. "It's fine. Believe me, I've been confronted before."

"We all have a busy day ahead of us. Why don't you try and get some rest. Excuse me," Katie said as she slipped out the conference room.

ALEXANDRIA SAT IN HER chrome chair, stroking Divinity, who rested in the palm of her hand.

"Go get some sleep, Katie."

"I wish I could, but I have this really unsettled feeling inside."

"Maybe you ate too many s'mores."

"Maybe I feel like my team is not all focused on the task at hand. Maybe I feel like my team is not a team right now." Alexandria ignored the comments. "Alex, I don't think for one minute that Linda Jordan is safe. At least not until that manuscript is delivered into the hands of her publishers. She's entrusted us to do that and I would sleep a whole lot better tonight if I thought everyone was behind that goal."

"What do you want from me, Katie?"

"I want you to put your personal feelings aside, be professional, and get onboard."

"You don't understand."

"What don't I understand?"

"What it's like."

"Really? You seemed to have forgotten one thing, Alex."

"What's that?"

"That I'm a survivor, too." Katie touched her stomach where the bullet fired from a drug lord's gun ripped through her abdomen and tore her uterus apart. "You're not the only person in this place that ever had to fight for her life," she said as she walked out.

Katie slept restlessly under a brown chenille throw. She had grown used to sleeping beside Joe the last few months, and several times now she woke up reaching for him. It wasn't until just before her watch shift was about to begin that she finally fell into a deep sleep.

She had the nightmare yet again, though they had become less frequent since she and Joe were seeing each other.

As always, it started with that sound of the magazine being racked back, the slide and click that broke the silence of the night. She felt him grab her by the hair and pull her close to him, suddenly aware of his scent, a combination of sweat and a musky cologne that seemed to be battling against each other for space. She heard him shout out, "She'll get it if anyone moves." She remembered seeing the movement out of the corner of her eye as one of her backups, crouched on all fours behind a trash can, shifted to get a better shot. She felt the barrel of the gun jammed into her rib cage and wondered if it was against a rib or between them. She heard the sound, almost as if someone had slowed it down, as he pulled the trigger and felt not pain, but a burning sensation of heat as the bullet ripped through her flesh and tore through her stomach. She remembered thinking about Joe and her mother—how hard it would be for them to get the news.

"Katarina, darling," Marcus said as he gently touched Katie's shoulder and gave it a nudge. Caught in her dreamlike state, Katie grabbed for his hand and twisted it around to try and throw him off balance. She flailed at him with her other arm, but it was caught up underneath the blanket.

"Holy Amazon," Marcus said as he tried to pull away from her.

"Katie, it's okay," she heard Antoine say, as he quickly knelt down in between them and shook her. "Katie, it's okay. Wake up."

Katie, who was breathing heavily, opened her eyes, saw them both standing there and blinked several times as she tried to regain her bearings. She let go of Marcus' hand and pulled her sweat-soaked shirt away from her skin.

"Are you okay?" Antoine whispered.

Katie sat up. "I'm fine."

Antoine helped her up to her feet. She looked around at the others, who were all sleeping.

"And you wonder why I don't sleep with women," Marcus whispered loudly as he rubbed at his arm.

"I told you I could take you, Marcus," Katie whispered back. Marcus backed away from her with a very tentative look.

"THERE," KATIE SAID AS she looked at the two women side by side.

"It's amazing," Linda said as she looked up and down at Jane, who was dressed in exactly the same outfit; an off-the-shelf pair of tan capri pants, a knit red shirt, and matching red straw hat.

"And for the ultimate touch," Katie said as she wrapped the fake silver fob around Jane's neck.

"Everyone knows what they have to do, right?" she asked looking around. They all nodded. "We'll meet up with Marcus and Antoine shortly. Portville, here we come." Katie reached around and double-checked that her weapon was secured in the holster. Just as she did so, they heard a loud tone indicating nearby motion from the exterior sensors.

Everyone froze.

"Bring it up on screen," Katie instructed Alexandria, who focused in on the camera that detected the motion. Katie looked at the car that was now parked in the back lot, next to her own.

"What the hell is she doing here?" Margo asked.

"Damn it," Katie said quietly.

"You want me to go kick her skinny ass out of here?" Margo asked, hands on hips.

Katie watched as the woman approached the front door. "It won't do any good," she said.

Chelsea Mattox rang the buzzer several times.

"Let her in, Janie," Katie said.

"But Katie," Jane began to protest, as she looked toward the others for support, "We're on our way..."

"It won't matter. Let her in."

Jane shrugged her shoulders as she walked out toward the front doors and let Chelsea Mattox in.

Katie glanced anxiously at her watch.

"You want me to stay back and tie her up for a few hours?" Margo asked. "If I sit on her, she won't be going anywhere."

"Thanks for the offer, Margo, but I don't think... Why, hello, Chelsea."

Chelsea Mattox barged in, paused for only one second as she glanced between the two identically clad women. Ignoring Jane completely, Chelsea strode toward Linda Jordan and extended her hand. "Miss Jordan, I've been looking forward to meeting you. I had a feeling you were here."

Linda paused. "But how did you...?"

"Linda, this is the reporter I was telling you about, Chelsea Mattox." The two women shook hands. Katie looked at her watch again. "Unfortunately, Chelsea, we have to be somewhere. I'm sure if you leave your business card, Linda will contact you very soon."

"Yes, I'd be happy to," Linda offered.

"No," Chelsea said very matter-of-factly as she spun around and faced Katie. "We had a deal. I get an exclusive interview and in return, I don't spill the beans on your operation."

"And no one says that can't happen, it's just that we're very pressed for time right now," Katie tried again.

"Too bad. I'm on deadline myself. I can either write about the renowned but reclusive author and promote her latest project, or I can write the story of my career about a group of misfit women who think they're spiders and their shady methods of operation."

"Did she just call us misfits?" Margo muttered under her breath. "'Cause I'll show you what a misfit looks like by shoving your skinny little ass …"

"Margo!" Katie said sharply. Katie turned back to Chelsea and held up her arm in a gesture of surrender. "Chelsea, work with me here. We need to leave now. Give us three hours, four at the most, and you'll get your interview."

Chelsea Mattox shook her head. "No deal. I get the interview now or never."

Katie turned around and looked at the others. "Could you all give us a minute, please?" she asked as the women retreated to the Cybercision room.

GLANCING ANXIOUSLY AT HER watch, Katie waited until the women had left and whipped around to face Chelsea.

"Don't take this personally, Chelsea, but you're getting to be a real sore under my thumb."

"I want that interview."

"Understood, but despite our … personal history … together, I at least thought you were a reasonable person. We need to be somewhere and you're not getting that."

"I have to have this interview."

"Why?"

Katie watched as Chelsea's dark eyes darted around the room then dropped to her feet.

"Something happened and I need to get this interview to make it all right."

"What happened?"

Chelsea's nostrils flared as she took a deep breath in and out.

"Someone nearly destroyed my career."

Katie acted as casually as she could at this bit of news.

"First my identity was stolen and I had fraudulent credit card charges appearing everywhere, then my name started showing up all over the Internet on stories I hadn't written and I nearly got canned until they figured out it wasn't me."

"Really?" Katie asked innocently. "That's your problem, not mine."

"Actually, I think it is your problem, too, except I haven't been able to prove it yet, but I will …"

"That's a pretty big accusation you're making, Chelsea. You'd better have evidence to back it up."

"Like I said, in time …"

"You go around making an accusation like that and I'll sue you and your paper for defamation of character, libel, slander, and whatever the hell else I can muster up, and then when they cut you loose and you're out on the street, you'll wish to hell you did have a new identity. Am I clear on that?"

"Fine, but we had a deal, Mahoney, unless your word means nothing."

Katie sighed and shook her head.

Chelsea stepped forward. "No one has been able to get near Linda Jordan. An exclusive would do a lot to restore my reputation and integrity."

Katie turned away from her and brought the other women back in.

"It's your call," she said quietly to Linda Jordan.

"I could always use the publicity."

KATIE KEPT A CLOSE eye on the side and rearview mirrors of her SUV as she drove. Alexandria sat beside her in front. Linda Jordan and Chelsea Mattox sat in the back seat. Margo and Jane were in the white Divinity Florals van with Margo driving, a few cars back.

"Have you completed the sequel?" Chelsea Mattox asked.

"Yes. That's where we're headed…"

"… to celebrate," Katie quickly interrupted. "We're going to celebrate its completion," Katie said, as she gave Linda an imploring glance.

"So you've already turned the manuscript over to the publishers?"

"Well, we…"

"I take it you're aware there was a two-million-dollar bounty to get hold of the manuscript? How do you feel about that?"

"It was quite disturbing. After all, I meant no harm by the story. As I was just saying last night, the book has raised a great deal of awareness about, and money for, cancer research."

Alexandria stared straight ahead. Katie noticed a dark-colored sedan abruptly change lanes, and nodded at Alexandria in the mirror.

"Do you expect the sequel to be as successful as *The Franklin Cure,* and can you tell me what it's about?"

"I can't tell you too many of the details, but I will say that the story picks up just as *The Franklin Cure* ends, and it further explores the controversy surrounding experimental drugs. It also furthers the romance between the two lead characters."

Katie picked up her cell phone.

"What's up?" Margo asked. "That little white bitch still practicing random acts of journalism?"

"Watch out for the dark-colored sedan coming up behind you."

"You want me to speed up?"

"No. I want you to slow down and make sure he gets a good look at your passenger."

"Huh?"

"Trust me. Let him see Janie, and then take him for a nice ride."

"Where do you want me to lead him to?"

"There's a state police barracks a few exits up. Take him for a tour there."

"I'm on it."

KATIE SHUT HER CELL phone. Chelsea began to turn around to look out the back window.

"Don't," Katie instructed her.

Chelsea ignored her and looked back anyway. She saw the white van with Margo driving and Jane in the bright red straw hat, seated next to her. Turning back, she looked at the silver fob around Linda Jordan's neck.

"You're on your way to deliver it now, aren't you?"

"Amazing," Katie said sarcastically to Alexandria, "it not only talks, it thinks occasionally, too." Alexandria grinned slyly.

"This is perfect," Chelsea announced, unperturbed. "It's like history in the making."

"Oh no," Katie said. "You've had your interview and the first chance we get, we'll drop you off and you can go on your merry way."

Katie watched in the rearview mirror as the sedan pulled up directly beside the van. Jane fingered the silver fob and stared straight ahead just as Katie had instructed her to. Margo suddenly sped up and passed a car. The black sedan immediately sped up, too.

"Good. They've taken the bait," Katie said.

"Will they be okay?" Linda asked with great concern in her voice. "I'd feel absolutely terrible if anything happened to them."

"The state police barracks is just down the road and we'll let them know they're on their way."

Katie quickly punched in a number and notified the dispatcher about a black car driving erratically and following a white van with two women in it.

"That will keep them busy for a few minutes," she said as she watched the black sedan race and weave through traffic to catch up to the van. She picked up her speed to stay ahead of them. At the next exit, Margo abruptly switched lanes and took the exit toward the police barracks. Without hesitation, the black sedan switched lanes and followed right behind her.

"THEY'VE GOT HIM," KATIE said a few minutes later as she closed her cell phone. "It was our mutual friend, Mr. Donahue again." Glancing in the rearview mirror toward Chelsea, Katie said, "Friend of yours?"

Chelsea Mattox flipped back her long black hair. "I don't know what you're talking about."

"He already told me you knew each other."

"We may have dated a few times. So what?"

"Was that before or after you decided to date my husband?"

Linda Jordan raised her eyebrows as the two women glared at each other via the rearview mirror. Katie suddenly veered wildly into the other lane, sending Chelsea Mattox, who was the only one not wearing her seat belt, sliding across the seat into the passenger door.

"Oops, sorry about that. Unexpected traffic. You okay, Linda?"

Linda Jordan sounded alarmed as she replied, "Yes, I think so."

"Call Antoine and tell him we're switching to Plan B with an extra passenger."

"You really want to take her along?" Alexandria asked.

"Not really, but I can keep a better eye on her if she's nearby. I don't trust her one bit if she's running around out there loose."

"Ah, halloooo, I can hear everything you're saying, you know."

"Goody for you."

KATIE PULLED THE CAR up to the marina and parked in the first available slot.

"Let's go, quickly!" she ordered. Alexandria slipped behind the wheel of the driver's seat.

"You know the plan, right?" Katie asked.

"I'm on it," Alexandria said as she pulled away.

"What is this?" Chelsea asked. "You're going by boat?"

"You continue to amaze me. What gave it away? Was it the water or all the seagulls?"

Katie led them hurriedly toward *The FlameBoyant* where Antoine and Marcus waited aboard for them. Marcus sipped a tall pink drink that had an umbrella floating on the top.

"An unexpected guest?" he said as he glanced up and down at Chelsea.

"Not by choice, believe me," Katie replied.

Marcus held up his ring-laden hand. "How do you do, I'm Marcus," he said quite formally.

"Don't bother with niceties, Marcus. Let's just get rolling," Katie said as she anxiously glanced all around. "We have just enough time to get there."

"My, my," Marcus said tsking at her. "I didn't realize this cruise was onboard the PMS *Princess Line*."

"I'm not in the mood for your flattery, Marcus."

Antoine nodded, cast off, and began to ease the boat out of its slip.

"You know the way?" Katie asked.

"North."

"Very funny."

"We'll tie up at the marina just down the road from their of-fices. You can see the building from the pier and can literally walk down the road to get there."

"Good."

Katie remained vigilant, relaxing only slightly when they got out on the open water. There were few boats around.

Marcus slipped his sunglasses down and peered at Linda Jor-dan. "No offense, Miss Linda, but one would think with all the cha-ching you made on that delightful tale of yours, that you could afford a bit more haute couture and something less…," he said, touching her knit shirtsleeve, "retail."

"I was the one who bought the outfits, Marcus," Katie ex-plained, "and yes, they're from a chain store, but I needed two and I needed them fast. So if you're going to send out the fashion po-lice, send them out after me."

"Katarina, darling, if the fashion police ever caught up with you and your Fashion's End wear, I'm afraid you'd be put away for a long, long time." Turning to Chelsea Mattox and touching her brown striped skirt, he said, "Now this I like. Armani?"

"Yes."

"You carry it well." Marcus smoothed his black silk pants. "These are Armani as well. They had a sale going on at Gay-Mart."

Katie rolled her eyes and shook her head.

"And for the record," Marcus continued, "I simply shudder at the thought of there being two of these polyester-blended atrocities running around," he said as he touched Linda's capris. "No offense meant, Miss Linda."

"Of course not."

"Speaking of which," Katie said, turning to Chelsea, "I'm curious about something. How is it that you knew which one was the real Linda Jordan?"

Chelsea tossed back her dark hair and smiled smugly. "That's easy. Linda Jordan has her ears double pierced. Your friend only has one set of piercings."

Katie refused to admit that she was impressed.

"You know, Marcus," Linda said in Katie's defense, "I do like to dress comfortably, too, when I'm writing."

"Miss Linda, there's a huge difference between comfort and panache and comfort and drab. No offense, Katarina, darling, but Annie Hall went out in the seventies."

Katie scowled at Marcus, particularly since Chelsea Mattox seemed to be enjoying the exchange, turned and looked out across the water. Far in the distance, she saw movement. A boat, and if she wasn't mistaken, a cigarette boat, bobbed along and was moving quickly in their direction.

Katie quietly touched Antoine on the arm and gestured.

"I see it," he said.

"What do you think?"

"At the rate they're going," Antoine said, "we'll know in just a few minutes if it's the same one."

"I don't suppose you have a cloaking device on board this thing?" Katie asked.

"On a boat called *The FlameBoyant*? Not hardly. Besides, that sounds like the kind of gadget you and your Black Widows ought to have," Antoine replied.

"Left the cloaking device and the can of invisible spray back at the office, darn it," Katie said. Snapping her fingers, she said, "Guess it's time for Plan C."

"What's Plan C?"

"I'll let you know as soon as I think of it."

"Is everything alright?" Linda asked hesitantly.

"Unfortunately, no. It appears we're going to have more company in a few minutes," Katie said as she nodded with her head toward the boat that was now much closer.

"Is that—?"

"It may very well be. How in the world did they know we were going to be …?" Katie began to say, but stopped and looked at Chelsea Mattox. Chelsea quickly turned away. Without saying another word, Katie swung around to where Chelsea was seated and shoved her hand into her jacket pocket.

"Hey!" Chelsea protested. "What the hell do you think you're doing?"

Katie dug into the front pocket, as Chelsea tried to pull her hand away.

"Would you two girls like to go down below and be alone?" Marcus asked watching them.

Katie came up with a cell phone.

"Give that back to me!" Chelsea demanded.

Katie flipped open the cell phone and looked at the display. "She's been broadcasting our location the whole time with the built in GPS. Damn it," she said as she took the shiny phone and tossed it as far as she could into the ocean.

"Now that's what I call long distance," Marcus commented. "Can you hear me now?"

"Hey!" Chelsea screamed as she stood up and grabbed Katie by the arm. "I needed that."

Katie pushed Chelsea's hands away. "I'm losing my patience with you, Chelsea. Now, tell me who that is," she said, pointing toward the cigarette boat as it got closer.

"I don't know what you're talking about."

"Bullshit. Who is it?"

"It's … it's not what you think."

Katie grabbed Chelsea Mattox by the hair and yanked her head back. "Listen to me, you little bitch, I've just about had it with you. You've been a thorn in my side since the day you walked into my life. I hold you personally responsible for the hole in my gut, do you hear me? I could care less if you end up being shark bait, but I do care about these other people. So either you start talking or take your chances that you're a real good swimmer," Katie added, as she dragged Chelsea toward the side of the boat.

"I'll have you arrested for assault!" Chelsea screamed as she tried to free herself from Katie's arms.

"First of all, you need witnesses for that, and I don't see anyone around here who would testify against me. Second, someone already tried to hurt Linda and my mother and I don't like anyone messing with my family. Third, Linda is a writer, a real writer, and unlike you, she has worked hard for two solid years to finish that book, and I'm not about to let you stop it from being published. Do you see where I'm coming from now? It's sink or swim time. You decide," Katie said as she pushed Chelsea farther toward the edge. The two women struggled while the others, choosing not to intervene, looked on.

"Holy Liza Minnelli," Marcus said dryly, "I had no idea there would be entertainment onboard this cruise. Shame there's no mud…"

"You touch me again and I'll find a way to prove it was you and your spider friends who stole my identity and destroyed my reputation."

Alexandria glanced momentarily at Katie, who immediately gave a small shake of her head, while loosening her grip ever so slightly on Chelsea.

"It's not what you think," Chelsea said. "They're here to protect her."

"What?"

"It's the people from the same company that Steve Donahue works for."

"Seamus Security?"

"Yes. They have a vested interest in making sure she and that silver thing get to the publishers intact. So you can stop being paranoid. They won't hurt anyone."

Katie mulled this over before releasing Chelsea, who tugged at her tight skirt and sat back down.

"Who told you this?"

"Steve."

"And you believed him?"

"Why shouldn't I?"

"So you deliberately arranged to be with us so they would know where she was?"

"What's the matter, Mahoney, can't stand the fact that you've been one-upped?"

KATIE WAS ABOUT TO reply as the cigarette boat approached their stern. She had an uneasy feeling in her stomach as she watched the boat come alongside theirs. Antoine put *The FlameBoyant* in neutral and the two boats bobbed next to each other in rhythm to the waves.

Though she had only seen him once before, the profile of the man driving the cigarette boat appeared identical to the man who had, just days earlier, sailed over the stern of Linda Jordan's boat, *The End*. Katie hoped she was wrong about that. There was no question, however, as to the identity of the other man seated next to the boat's pilot.

"Well, well, if it isn't Katie Mahoney!" the man called as he reached across and grabbed the rail of *The FlameBoyant*. "Permission to come aboard, Captain?" Eddie Seamus asked Antoine. Antoine looked to Katie.

"You'd better have a damned good explanation for all this, Eddie," Katie said as she reached out and grabbed the railings to allow him to board.

EDDIE SEAMUS WAS OF average height, with a stocky build. He'd put on a lot of weight since leaving the force. His once jet-black hair was thinned and styled in an awful comb-over. That, along with his bulbous nose, gave him a bizarre resemblance to W.C. Fields. He was reputed to spend every night at the local cop bar, The Blue Line, owned by Katie's former partner, Sean McCleary. Katie had heard many stories from Sean about Eddie Seamus and his uncontrollable affection for Jameson. Many times, Sean had to call a cab or get one of the local guys to take Eddie, who was too wasted to walk back home under his own power.

"Top of the morning to you all," Eddie Seamus said. "Eddie Seamus of Seamus Security and an old pal of Katie's. Sorry for the intrusion but I've got business here," he said, glancing quickly at the silver fob around Linda Jordan's neck. "Miss Jordan, it's an honor," Eddie said as he shook Linda Jordan's hand.

"What kind of business?" Katie asked as she eyed the boat's pilot in the black wetsuit.

"I'm under contract with Ryan & Rogers to see to it that that," he said, pointing toward Linda's neck, "gets delivered safely."

"Well, I'm afraid your services are no longer needed because we're under contract now."

"Really? Who hired you?" Eddie asked.

"I did," Linda said.

Eddie Seamus glanced around as if he were sizing them all up. "My orders are to take that silver thing and deliver it in person."

"How interesting since no one, including Linda, ever heard of such an order."

"Forgive the subterfuge, but her publishers, Ryan & Rogers, didn't want her to know for fear she'd be so frightened she couldn't finish the book."

Katie studied him for several seconds. "Who's your driver, Eddie?"

"That's Buck. Ex-Army Ranger."

"Where was he the other day when Linda almost got killed by someone wearing a black wetsuit in a cigarette boat?"

Eddie, who had been grinning widely, narrowed his smile. "Can't say. Look, Katie, you know me better than that."

"I sure do, which is exactly why I'm asking."

Eddie shrugged. "Business is business," he said.

"Yeah, and scaring potential clients into thinking they actually need security is a lousy way to get it."

"What? Aw, come on, Katie, you don't think…"

"That's exactly the kind of strong-armed tactics you were famous for at the PD, Eddie. I bet you arranged the entire episode so Linda would be scared enough to tell Ryan & Rogers what was going on, and they'd keep you under contract."

Eddie felt every pair of eyes staring at him and glanced anxiously away.

"Except," Katie went on, "your friend Buck went a little overboard, excuse the expression, and almost drowned her."

"What?" Linda asked, as she rose slightly from her seat. "Is this true?"

"You're full of shit, Katie," Eddie Seamus said. "You were always full of shit. And who the hell are you to judge me? You got canned from the job, too."

"I got canned trying to protect an innocent woman from being sent to jail. Big difference, Eddie."

"The past is the past. For now, we'll take care of getting that to the publishers," he said as he stepped forward.

Katie pulled out her cell phone and handed it to Linda Jordan. "Call them," she said. "Tell Ryan & Rogers that we've been slightly delayed and ask them if all of this is true."

"Now hold on a minute, Katie," Eddie Seamus began to say. He glanced back at the man on the other boat and gestured with his head. "I won't have anyone second guessing me like that. I'm a professional."

The man on the other boat suddenly stood up and it was then that Katie noticed the black butt of a semi-automatic handgun sticking out of a holster strapped to his waist.

"Back your goon off," Katie said, "or I'll personally toss the damn thing in the ocean."

Eddie waved a hand at the man, but it did little to make Katie feel any better.

"Make the call," she instructed Linda.

Linda Jordan had just dialed and said, "Carly? It's Linda," when Eddie Seamus abruptly reached forward, grabbed the cell phone from her hands, and tossed it in the water.

"Now the fish can chat with each other," Marcus observed.

Katie turned back to see Buck standing with his weapon trained on them.

"Give it to me," Eddie Seamus declared, as he withdrew his own weapon from his ample waist and pointed it at Linda Jordan.

"You lousy son of a …," Katie began to say, but Eddie Seamus waved the gun around so wildly that she was afraid he would shoot them all.

"I said, give it to me."

"You plan on killing us all, Eddie? There are others who know of your involvement."

"I'm not planning on killing anyone. And as for the other people, try and find me. Two million will let me hide very nicely for quite some time. Now give me the damn necklace."

Katie planted herself in between Eddie Seamus and Linda Jordan. She was more worried about Buck, who seemed much steadier on his feet and probably a better shot than Eddie, who swayed every time the boat rocked.

"You set this whole thing up, didn't you?"

"I've got news for you, Katie, but I really was hired by those people."

"And what? You didn't like the pay scale?"

"You figure it out. I could deliver this thing to them for five thousand or deliver it to someone else for two million."

"You almost got nothing when she went overboard."

"A slight tactical error on Buck's part. He was simply supposed to frighten her."

"So you sold your soul to the devil. Shame on you, Eddie."

"I'll remember to do penance while I'm basking in the sun on my own private beach."

"What are you going to do? Shoot me to get to her?"

"If necessary," Eddie said as he shoved Katie aside with his hand and grabbed for the necklace.

"Ow!" Katie heard Linda yell as she tried to protect her neck. Chelsea Mattox stood up behind her and tried to grab the necklace from behind. Katie could not tell if she was trying to protect Linda's neck, or grab the fob.

"Oh, no you don't," Katie said, as she immediately stood up and joined the fracas. Antoine struggled to get to them as the boat began to rock from side to side from all the on-board motion, but kept losing his balance. Marcus remained seated, watching the action.

Eddie Seamus grabbed hold of Katie's arm and tried to pull her away with one arm, while trying to grab the silver fob with the other.

A pile of arms and hands wrestled for possession of the shiny silver fob as the boat began to rock wildly from side to side from all the commotion.

In the midst of all of them grabbing for the silver fob, the clasp of the chain suddenly snapped apart and it, along with the silver fob, landed soundly in Marcus' lap.

"Grab it, Marcus!" Katie yelled.

"I'll split the two million with you," Eddie Seamus yelled even louder.

Marcus picked the silver fob and chain up and stared at them all as they shouted and yelled his name. They suddenly were all silenced by the sound of a lone gunshot echoing across the water. Everyone stopped and turned toward Buck.

"Good boy," Eddie said to Buck as he broke free. "Now give it to me," he ordered Marcus.

"Actually," Buck said, speaking for the first time, "I'll do fine with that on my own," he said as he trained his gun on them all, including Eddie Seamus. "Toss that over on my boat nice and easy," he commanded Marcus.

Marcus remained frozen, unsure of what to do.

"Do it, or this one," he said, pointing the gun at Antoine, "gets it first."

"Buck!" Eddie Seamus said. "I treated you like you were my own son. Like family. I gave you a job when no one else would."

"Well here's a news flash for you, Pops. I'm sick and tired of working for a two-bit, has-been drunk. I have my own islands to get to. Now toss it over here, Queer Head."

Katie saw Marcus' shoulders stiffen.

"What did you just call me?" he said, staring at the man.

"You heard me. Toss it here, Fag, or your friend gets it first."

Marcus took a deep breath and Katie watched his nostrils flare ever so slightly.

"Mr. Seamen," Marcus said, turning to Eddie, "though I love the tight black ensemble, I find your friend rather offensive."

"Just toss it. Now!" Buck screamed as he trained the weapon on Antoine.

"GIVE IT TO HIM," Linda Jordan said quietly. "I don't care anymore. I don't want anyone getting hurt or killed over it. Just give it to him."

"IF YOU CAN'T HAVE it, Miss Linda," Marcus began, "then no one can." They watched in disbelief as Marcus cocked his arm back and flung the silver fob as far as he could. As if in slow motion, the small silver fob arced high above both boats and landed with a small "plop" on the water's surface. The waterproof case kept it buoyant and it was only because of the strong reflection of the sun that they could see the tiny fob glistening on the surface like a silvery jewel in a swirl of darkness.

Katie turned to Linda Jordan and saw the unbelieving look in her eyes as she watched her manuscript, two years of her life, bob up and down in the Atlantic Ocean.

Buck was the first one in the water. He dove over the side of the cigarette boat and began swimming hard toward the fob. Antoine stripped his T-shirt off and dove in next. Both men raced toward the floating object whose reflection beamed back at them like a signal beacon.

"To your left!" Katie screamed as Antoine appeared to go off course. Antoine's strong strokes were equal to Buck's, but the wet-suit gave Buck the advantage and Katie could tell that Antoine was feeling the effects of the cold ocean water despite it being summer. Nonetheless, Antoine swam on and pumped his arms and legs furiously as he tried to get closer to the fob, which was being carried away from both men by the waves.

Suddenly, the fob began to twist around in strange circles.

"What in mercy's name is that?" Marcus asked as he watched it circle round, go under the water, rise up, and go back under again. They all waited several seconds to see if it would rise back up but it did not.

Antoine and Buck both stopped swimming and paddled around in circles to try and see where it had gone. Antoine looked back toward Katie, who shrugged her shoulders and shook her head. Antoine swam quickly back toward the boat.

"What happened?" Linda asked as Katie and Marcus hauled Antoine back on board.

"Something got it," Antoine said, in between breaths. He was shivering and Katie grabbed towels from under the seat and tossed them to Marcus, who wrapped them around Antoine.

"It must have been a blue or a striper. The fob looked enough like a lure."

KATIE DREW HER WEAPON on Eddie Seamus.

"You have one minute to get the hell out of my sight, Eddie," she said.

"No harm meant, Katie," Eddie Seamus said as he quickly climbed back on board the cigarette boat. Buck was still in the water.

"And this one will need a ride back," Katie said as she gestured toward Chelsea Mattox.

"But the story," Chelsea began.

"There is no story," Katie said reluctantly.

Eddie held out his hands to Chelsea Mattox as she climbed over.

"Eddie!" Buck called desperately from the water. "Eddie, please, I didn't mean it. I would have split the money with you, I swear!"

Eddie Seamus allowed Buck to beg several more times before letting him climb back aboard. Without another glance, the three took off in the opposite direction.

LINDA JORDAN SANK ONTO the plastic-covered seat. She looked pale.

"Are you okay?" Katie asked.

Linda stared back out over the water where the fob had landed.

"I am sorry, Miss Linda," Marcus said, leaning forward toward her. "You really didn't want those ugly people to have it, did you?"

"No, of course not. It's all right, Marcus. I just need a little time." Her voice sounded vapid.

"Linda, I'm so sorry," Katie said, as she sat down next to her.

"Perhaps I can write it again," Linda said, but she gave Katie such an imploring look that Katie knew that would never happen.

Antoine rose and slipped his shirt back on.

"Are you okay?" Katie asked.

"I'm fine. I'm just sorry I couldn't get there in time."

"Seems like you're always diving in deep water for me," Linda said. "Thank you for trying."

"What now?"

"They're all still waiting for us," Katie said. Antoine took his position behind the helm and pushed the throttle forward.

"Here you go, Miss Linda," Marcus said, as he handed her a glass of brandy.

"Thank you. If no one minds, I think I'll go down below for a few minutes."

"Of course," Katie said sympathetically.

Linda stopped at the bulkhead. "I know this is hard to understand, but there's very little difference between writing a book and bringing up a child. You conceive of the idea, labor over it for months and months, it emerges and you mold it and shape it, and try to make it the best it can be, knowing full well that others will judge you by it, and forever connect you to it." She looked back out toward the water. "I can't help but feel my child just drowned."

MARCUS WAS REMARKABLY SUBDUED and contrite the whole way up to Portville.

"What are you drinking, Marcus?" Katie asked, trying to cheer him up, but he didn't answer, just continued to stare out across the water.

Antoine beckoned to Katie. "Just keep the wheel steady," he said to her as she took over his position and he knelt down beside Marcus.

"I would have done the same thing," Antoine said soothingly to his partner as he rubbed his arm. "You were trying to protect me and not let them get the book," Antoine said, but Marcus remained silent.

THEY ARRIVED AT THE Portville pier. Antoine and Katie took Linda Jordan under either arm because she was still a bit unsteady. Marcus followed behind in silence.

"What will I tell them?" she asked.

"Just tell them the truth."

"They've invested so much in me."

"Remember you're still a very successful author. They'll invest in you again when the next book comes along."

"With all that has happened," Linda said quietly, "I'm not so sure there'll be a next time. Perhaps I'll just retire with the earnings from *The Franklin Cure* and catch up on some reading."

"What?" Marcus asked from behind. "Miss Linda, you can't give up being a writer anymore than I could wake up tomorrow loving baseball and swigging beer. It's what you are."

Linda Jordan reached back and took Marcus' hand.

"Thank you, Marcus."

"Can you imagine this coiffure," Marcus said patting his head, "jammed under a baseball cap? I think not."

"Come on," Katie said, "they're expecting us."

THE WALLS OF RYAN & ROGERS' offices were lined with posters touting *The Franklin Cure* and articles about Linda Jordan, including framed shots of her on the front covers of *Newsweek* and *Time* magazines. Alexandria, Margo, and Jane were all sitting in the front waiting room while another woman, around Katie's age, paced back and forth and talked on her cell phone.

"The press release will be out within the next twenty-four hours," the woman sporting sneakers, jeans, and a gauzy shirt said. Her long, brown hair was pulled straight back in a knot and she twisted a silver stylus around in one hand like a baton, occasionally tapping on a PalmPilot while she balanced the phone against her shoulder. She glanced up and smiled broadly at Linda Jordan. "Just tell them to standby and we'll give you as much as we can. I'll also forward a media kit and the stills from the movie and we'll set up the press conferences shortly. Gotta go," she said as she flipped the phone closed.

"Linda!" she said as she came forward with a big hug.

"Carly, this is Katie Mahoney of the Black Widow Agency. Katie, this is Carly Ryan, co-owner of Ryan & Rogers."

"You're with these ladies?" Carly said, glancing at Margo and Jane.

"Yes."

"That was Derek," Carly said. "My husband, Derek Rogers," she explained. "He's in Hollywood watching the shooting. He's been hobnobbing with celebrities all day. I told him he'd better not forget where Portville is and fall for some starlet. Well, Linda, you seem to have brought quite an entourage with you."

"I hired them, Carly, to protect …," Linda began, but plopped down on the couch without finishing the sentence.

Margo sidled up to Katie and whispered, "Where's the damn necklace?" into her ear. Katie shook her head back and forth. Margo's mouth dropped open. Margo walked back over to the leather couch Jane and Alexandria were sitting on and whispered the news to them. Jane clutched at the fake silver fob she was wearing around her neck.

"Well, this is the moment we've all been waiting for," Carly said, unaware. "Ladies, you're all about to witness publishing history. Let's have it, Linda."

Linda Jordan looked toward Katie, who stepped forward. "You see, Carly, we ran into a bit of trouble out on the water and as you know, there was only one copy and …"

"Oh, my God," Carly Ryan said as she swept her hand to her chest. "Oh, my God, please don't tell me …"

"The thugs you hired …"

"It was my fault," Marcus said quietly from the corner.

"What?" Margo asked.

"I threw it in the ocean."

"What the hell did you do that for, Marcus?" Margo asked in an incredulous tone.

"Oh, my God, this can't be happening," Carly said again, and, for a minute, Katie thought she was going to pass out.

"Because he was going to shoot Antoine, that's why," Marcus said.

"It wasn't anyone's fault," Linda said. "At least not these people," she said gesturing to the Black Widow Agency staff. "And you," she said taking Marcus' hand, "were trying to save a loved one."

Antoine put his arm around Marcus. "You did save me, as far as I'm concerned."

"Why didn't someone go after it?" Jane asked.

"We did."

"I thought it was waterproof. Doesn't that mean it would float?"

"A fish got it," Antoine said.

"A fish?" Margo asked incredulously. "You mean to tell me a damn fish ate her forty million dollar book?"

"I think it was a shark. I'm quite certain I saw fins," Marcus added.

"It wasn't a shark, Marcus," Antoine assured him.

"If it was, that's the most expensive damned fish in the sea," Margo said.

"Please, you people are not making any sense," Carly Ryan implored as she clapped her hands. "What are you talking about with this fish. Linda," she said shaking her head, "do you have the manuscript or not? Please tell me you have it."

"I don't."

THE ROOM FELL SILENT. Katie watched the color drain from Carly Ryan's face. Her shoulders dropped, the cell phone rang and she just ignored it as she sank down like an old woman into a leather chair.

"You don't have it?" she said, asking again.

"No," Linda Jordan said.

"BUT I DO," A lone voice rang out. Everyone turned to Alexandria who was sitting alone on a chair in the corner.

"What?" Linda asked as she strode over to Alexandria. Carly Ryan immediately sat forward on her seat.

Alexandria reached into her pocket and pulled out an identical silver fob and dangled it at them.

"How could you?" Linda asked. "Is that the original?"

"No."

"But I never made any copies."

"You didn't have to."

"I don't understand."

"Was it the laptop?" Katie asked and Alexandria nodded.

"What Alexandria did," Katie explained, "was forensically recover the files from the laptop you used when you were typing the story."

"But I never saved the story on that laptop nor any other computer, just on that portable drive ..."

"It didn't matter. Every time you work on a file, the computer makes an image of it, whether you tell it to or not. Most word processing programs make automatic backups so the file can be recovered in the event it gets damaged or the machine abruptly shuts down. So whether or not you actually saved the manuscript didn't matter. The laptop saved it for you. When you went missing from my mother's place, I grabbed the laptop and brought it back to our forensics lab. Alex must have been able to recreate it in its entirety. Nice job, Alex. You saved the day."

Everyone broke out in applause.

"Holy Ethel Merman," Marcus declared. "If I wake up tomorrow yelling 'home run' and craving a Budweiser, someone slap me upside the head."

"I'd be happy to," Margo said under her breath.

"I have one thing I want to say," Alexandria began. "You already know that I felt your first book was dangerous. I think this one is, too; but I also believed you when you said that the book has raised awareness and consciousness and helped research. That's the only reason I'm doing this."

Alexandria handed the fob over to Linda Jordan, who clasped her hands around Alexandria's and held them. "You have no idea how grateful I am to you for this. You have my solemn word that I will work harder than anyone else to continue to promote that good work." Linda looked down at her hand and stared at the shiny silver fob.

"This calls for a celebration!" Carly Ryan announced.

HOURS LATER, THE FOUR women gathered back in the Black Widow Agency kitchen.

"I don't know about the rest of you," Margo began, "but I couldn't eat another bite and believe me, that's saying something."

"I've never had such wonderful, fresh seafood," Jane commented.

"I feel like I'm about to burst," Katie said, "but there is one thing we still need to do …" She reached down into their chiller and pulled out a bottle of champagne. Popping the cork, she poured four glasses and handed them out. "I would like to propose a toast," she said as they all raised their glasses. "To Jane for doing such a brave job as Linda's twin."

"Here, here."

"… And to Alex for setting her personal feelings aside to do the right thing. You came through, Alex."

"Amen to that," Margo said.

"Here, here," said Jane.

Just then, Alexandria's cell phone began to ring. "Hello? Sure, I'll be right there," she said as she set her glass back down. "Sorry, I need to go."

She left without saying another word.

"I still say she has some motherboard cyber lover tucked away somewhere and they digitally get down on each other," Margo conjectured.

"It is rather odd," Jane added, "that she disappears so. And it would be nice to think Alexandria had someone special in her life."

"Oh, she has someone special, alright," Katie said, and then glancing over her shoulder, she added, "I guarantee you she'll have a man in her arms in just a few minutes."

Margo and Jane stared at Katie as she walked out the door.

HOURS LATER, KATIE ROLLED over in her bed.

"You always do get worked up whenever weapons are drawn," Joe said, easing his long frame beside her.

"You were pretty worked up, yourself." Her hand glided down his chest.

"I'm getting used to this, you know," he said, running his hands through her hair.

"I know."

"Katie?"

"Yeah..."

"Do you ever think about what it would be like if we got together again?"

"Joe," she said, as she rolled back over on him, "we are together."

"Prove it," he said.

20

KATIE SLIPPED INTO THE cyber café Alexandria was known to frequent. She immediately spotted her in the back booth, her favorite spot. Katie watched as Alexandria's hands flew across the keyboard of the laptop propped open in front of her. Without looking up to acknowledge Katie's presence, Alexandria said, "Sit."

"I talked to my mother earlier. They all love the new computer that Linda sent over. Just think, they'll be able to download their porn a lot quicker now..."

Alexandria abruptly set the laptop aside.

"I volunteer at the hospital," she finally began. "I help the kids out by teaching them about computers. Most of them know more than... well... Jane, let's say. They're pretty savvy."

"That's amazing. I mean about what the kids know."

"Yes," Alexandria said quietly.

Katie waited patiently for her to speak again. When she didn't, Katie brought it up herself. "I bumped into someone in the hallway that day, a Dr. Davis." She watched and waited to see if Alexandria reacted, but she didn't. "He said most patients never want to come back."

Alexandria sipped her coffee very slowly, then cradled the cup with her long, thin fingers.

"Alex, look, I'm sorry. I had no idea …," Katie began.

"I didn't want anyone to know."

"Why?"

"Because you get treated differently."

"I won't ask you to tell me anymore than what you're willing to share, but I do have to ask you one thing. Are you okay? Now, I mean?"

"I'm fine, Katie. I've been fine for years."

"I'm so relieved to hear that."

They sat in silence for a few minutes. Katie was about to get up and leave when Alexandria spoke.

"I WAS TEN YEARS old. It was one of the more common forms of childhood leukemia, so there were a lot of treatment options available to me. I practically lived at Laketon General for seventeen months while I underwent a series of treatments. I hated the needles. Before anyone would stick me, they'd always touch me and say, 'This will be just a small prick and won't hurt,' but it did. It hurt. They all lied about it. They touched me and they lied. In some ways, that was worse than the treatment and the sickness itself. That and the fact that I couldn't go to school. I couldn't be near any of my friends, the risk was too great that I'd pick something up from one of them. Sometimes, my parents weren't even allowed to come near me unless they put on gowns and masks.

"Someone donated a computer to the hospital. It was old, but I learned how to program it very quickly, and eventually I was able to hook into the hospital's network so I could use what was, back then, a very early version of the Internet. I joined bulletin boards, and because they didn't know how old I was, the others shared all kinds of tips and taught me things. I learned from the bottom up. The connection was excruciatingly slow, but I had nothing but time. It kept me going.

"Some used their knowledge for legitimate use, but there was a group of people, mostly guys, called The Backdoors. They were the first hacking group I ever met and they were smart. A lot smarter than the good guys."

"That's why you were making the donations to the children's funds when I arrested you?" Katie asked.

"Yes. The hospital desperately needs equipment, Katie. They need new computers and monitors, not for the hospital staff, but for the patients. You have no idea how quickly you can become isolated when you're getting treatments. Time seems to stand still and you want to tear your hair out, except you've usually lost it already.

"Having access to the Internet is powerful. It breaks down the doors and levels the playing field. No one knows you're sick when you're chatting with someone on the Internet unless you choose to tell them. That's the most important gift—to be accepted. And with some decent video equipment and a high-speed connection at both ends, these kids could be hooked back into their class-rooms and still be a part of their school, their friends' lives, their communities."

"I had no idea."

"Most people don't. Hopefully, most never will."

"But Antoine knew?"

"He lost someone close, too, once. A cousin. He just happened to mention it one day and we started talking…"

"It's okay," Katie interrupted. "You don't have to tell me."

"It's hard to explain. It's hard to grasp."

"I understand."

"There was another girl while I was there, around my age. She had a rarer form of leukemia. We became friends. Her family had no money. Her parents sold their house to try and pay for the medical bills, but the bills kept mounting and mounting. We're talking millions of dollars, Katie, for even the most common treatments and her treatments weren't common.

"I did my first hack when I was eleven and got into the hospital's billing department and very slowly reduced the balance on her account. I tried to teach her stuff on the computer, too, but she was too weak a lot of the time. She couldn't even hold up a book, but she liked to learn about things. She loved spiders. She said if she didn't make it, she'd come back as a spider…"

Alexandria paused.

"Her name was Divinity. Divinity Brown."

Katie let the words sink in for a few minutes before speaking.

"ALEX, I CAN'T IMAGINE what you went through. I just want you to know how sorry I am…"

"Don't be," Alexandria said. "I don't want anyone's sympathy. I have no need for it. I'm a survivor."

"You certainly are. Thanks for telling me," Katie said. "I won't tell anyone else."

Alexandria pulled her laptop back in front of her, signaling the end of the conversation.

Katie rose, then hesitated. "Hey, Alex?"

"What?"

"Thanks for being there for me when I needed you."

JANE SAT ON HER front porch, stroking her cat, Angel, as she finished the last few pages of Linda Jordan's newest best-selling novel, *The Cure Experimental*. Sighing with deep satisfaction, she flipped for the hundredth time to the dedication page and read the words yet again:

WITH LOVE, ALWAYS, TO *my incredible publishers, Ryan & Rogers, who proved that smaller is better. To my unexpected twin, Jane, thanks for stepping up when I needed you to. To Margo, thanks for the delightful and delicious sustenance. To Marcus, you kept it all in the right hands. Thanks. To my roommate, Molly, thanks for sharing Jack with me. To my real-life hero, Antoine, my deepest gratitude for pulling me from rough waters. To Katie, thanks for keeping me safe in your web. And finally, to Alexandria, thank you for giving me back what I almost lost...*

Jane grinned as the cat purred loudly and rubbed against Jane's arm.

"I know, Angel," she said glancing at her watch, "but Mommy has to go take care of something very important."

Margo's boyfriend, Cal, held a baseball mitt in one hand and her son, Trevor's hand in the other as Margo laced up her sneakers.

"Good luck at your ball game, sweetie," Margo said as she pulled his baseball cap down and tucked his jersey in his pants. "I'm sorry I can't be there today, but I have somewhere very important I need to be, but you have a good game, okay?"

"We'll whoop their damn asses," Trevor replied enthusiastically.

Margo raised her eyebrows, frowned and posted her hands on her ample hips. "Trevor Marcus Norton! I do not want to hear those words coming out of your mouth. Do you understand me?"

"Yes, ma'am," Trevor said remorsefully.

"Now go on outside and Cal will be right with you."

Trevor ran outside.

Cal could barely hold his laughter in.

"And what is so damn funny?" Margo asked.

"The boy has your spirit, that's all," Cal said as he leaned forward and kissed her on the cheek.

"Spirit, my damn ass. It's that damn school teaching him all that."

Cal smiled and placed his hands around her waist. "I like your spirit," he said and nuzzling her ear, he whispered, "I like a lot of other things, too."

The Black Widow Agency van pulled into the loading zone of the Laketon General Children's Hospital with Alexandria at the wheel. Katie and Margo, who had been awaiting its arrival, came out to meet it. Inside the van, stacked floor to ceiling, were boxes of new computers, new monitors, and new printers.

"Now how the hell are we supposed to get all of this inside?" Margo asked.

"They're bringing carts down," Alexandria said.

No sooner had she said it than the doors opened wide and a slightly stooped, silver-haired man—wearing a white coat, and a stethoscope with a bear attached to it around his neck, came out with a large push cart.

"Alex!" he said, beaming. Margo watched in shock as the man leaned forward and gave Alexandria a kiss on the cheek.

"This is Dr. Davis," Alexandria began. "This is my friend, Margo. She and some other friends are going to give us some help today."

"Good," Dr. Davis said, "because we'll need all the help we can get. I understand an entire tractor trailer will be pulling up momentarily."

"We'll get started with these first," Alexandria said, as she maneuvered the cart to the back of the van.

"The kids can't wait to see you, Alex," Dr. Davis said.

"You didn't tell them, did you? It was supposed to be a surprise…"

"I know, but little Andrew needed a lot of hope this morning. He's now looking forward to this afternoon. I didn't think you'd mind."

"Of course not."

Dr. Davis stopped them and touched Alexandria on the arm. "Alex, I can't thank you enough," he said. "I'd like to think this is the start of many miracles."

"You're welcome, but I'm not the one to thank. This has all been paid for by the Linda Jordan Foundation."

"And TBI Pharmaceuticals has teamed up with them to ensure that you will be well supplied with whatever medicine you need," Katie announced.

"It's unheard of," Dr. Davis said, shaking his head.

Katie immediately took charge.

"Okay, Margo, you grab that end, and Alex, you maneuver the cart over this way."

"Don't y'all be ordering me around like some damn servant or something," Margo complained as she hefted the first box onto the cart. "My people don't take kindly to being ordered around by white folks."

They had finished loading the first cart when they heard "Yoo-Hoo, darlings!" Turning, they saw Marcus and Antoine. Antoine was dressed casually in designer jeans and a Tommy Hilfiger T-shirt. Marcus looked like he was dressed for a Bahama cruise in an outrageous orange jungle-motif print shirt, flowing black silk pants, and sandals.

"Don't ask," Katie said quietly to Dr. Davis, who just looked at Marcus and smiled.

"The more, the merrier," he said.

"Oh, he's merry, alright," Katie replied.

"How the hell did you ever get my brother to volunteer for physical labor?" Margo asked Antoine.

"He thought I said the proctology department, not the oncology department," Antoine explained, and they all broke out in laughter.

"There you are, darlings!" Marcus said, strolling up behind him. "I am here to assist you," he said.

"Okay, Marcus," Katie said, "you can start with that next box."

Marcus frowned. "Box? Box? I'm afraid that isn't possible, sweetie," he said glancing at his hands. "I just had a manicure and was ordered to not touch anything for at least two hours."

Katie rolled her eyes. "Then what did you come here to do?" she asked.

"I'm here to provide support, Katarina darling," he explained. "Antoine, my Beloved, you're doing a wonderful job. Love those capris, Margo. Work them, Sister. Are you a doctor? Cute little bear. I'm having a problem with my left pinky toe. Perhaps you could take a look at it sometime. It sometimes points the wrong way…"

KATIE AND ANTOINE HOISTED several monitor boxes onto the next cart.

"Okay, what the hell is going on?" Margo asked as she yanked Katie by the arm and pulled her aside.

"What do you mean?"

"You know damn well what I mean," Margo said wagging her finger in Katie's face. "That doctor is all over our anorexic poster child, feeling her up, and saying the kids all want to see her. What's up with that?"

"Alexandria's family has helped out the Children's Hospital for years. Linda Jordan will get the publicity and some nice tax deductions, so it's win-win for both of them." She turned and winked to Antoine. "If only we could claim this deduction on our own business taxes," she added.

"And you can," said a voice from behind them. They all turned to see Jane.

"But we didn't donate the money," Katie said.

"No, but we are donating our time and that certainly counts for a deduction, especially at the hourly rates we bill."

JUST THEN, A SEMI-TRACTOR trailer truck backed up to the loading dock. The driver jumped off and lifted up the back gate, revealing dozens of huge boxes with all kinds of computer and video equipment.

"Oh dear," Jane said. "How are we ever going to get all of this unloaded?"

"Don't worry," Katie said, "I already took care of that," she said pointing as a silver van with "Police—Special Events Unit" pulled around the corner and swung into place nearby. The back door opened and about a dozen officers in civilian clothes jumped effortlessly out the back of the van. Joe Kennedy was the last off.

"Okay, people," he ordered, "you all know what to do. Let's get this stuff moved now!" The men and women began hoisting boxes down off the truck in fire brigade style, and passed box after box toward the empty carts waiting at the door. Joe came over and kissed Katie on the cheek.

"I see the cavalry has arrived," she said.

"Laketon PD at your service, ma'am."

Katie took one of his hands in hers and one of Margo's in the other. "Now, do you think you two can get along for just a day so we can help these kids out?"

"As long as it's just one day," Joe said, grinning.

Margo nodded. "It's gonna be a long damn day," she said, then shaking her head, she added, "but I suppose if he behaves..."

"Don't count on it," Joe said, with a twinkle in his eye.

MARCUS CLAPPED HIS HANDS excitedly as he watched all the action. "I've never seen such a joyous collection of pure testosterone all in one place before."

Joe bristled at the comment and fell into place beside Antoine, Margo, and Jane. They quickly had the first cart fully loaded.

"Third floor and left at the elevators," Katie announced.

"She loves to bark orders," Joe whispered to Antoine.

"So does Marcus," Antoine replied.

Katie started to go with them when she realized that Alexandria was still back at the van, standing motionless, watching the whole busy procession.

"Listen, guys, I'll catch up with you in a minute. We won't all fit on the elevator anyway," Katie said excusing herself. "Go on up."

She walked over to Alexandria.

"Hey, are you coming?"

Alexandria nodded.

"The kids will want to see you. It's you who should really be there, not us."

"I know," Alexandria said, very quietly.

"Alex, are you okay?"

Alexandria nodded again. It took her a long time to speak. "This is a dream," she finally said.

"No," Katie corrected her. "This is reality. And this one's for Divinity."

THE END

If you enjoyed *Spun Tales,* read on for an
except from the next book by Felicia Donovan,

Fragile Webs

COMING SOON FROM MIDNIGHT INK

"OKAY, NANCY DREW," MARGO Norton complained from the passenger's seat, "you want to give me a little clue as to what this big mystery is all about?"

"I told you," Katie Mahoney said as she whipped the Black Widow Agency's white surveillance van through downtown Laketon's entertainment district, "I'm taking you somewhere special. It's a surprise."

Margo eyed her suspiciously. "I'll remind you that one of your little surprises nearly landed my wide black ass behind bars once. And if you think I look good in stripes, try jamming an elephant into a zebra suit."

Katie laughed.

"Not to worry, Margo. No jail time where we're going."

"When you said, 'Don't make any plans for Friday night, it's going to be a special night for just the two of us,' what exactly did you mean?" Margo asked as she studied Katie with her wild strawberry-blonde hair squashed down underneath a Red Sox cap, pony-tail protruding in a bundle out the small opening in the back. Katie had traded in her trademark tight sweater and skirt, which normally hugged her feminine curves, for a man's button-down shirt that hung loosely off her shoulders, and a pair of jeans.

"You'd better not be taking me to no damn baseball game," Margo complained. "Bunch of grown men running around chasing after a damn ball. The only ball I want to play with when a man is involved is…"

"Relax, Margo," Katie said firmly. "I know you're not into sports."

"Not unless it involves Calvin," Margo said, referring to her boyfriend, "in which case I've been round all the bases many times," she said, blowing on her fingernails.

"Thanks for sharing," Katie said dryly. "Actually, I'm taking you out for a drink."

Margo cocked her head and eyed her suspiciously. "You're what?"

"You heard me. I said I'm taking you out for a drink. You've been working very hard lately…"

"You mean we're not working?"

"Technically, yes, we're working, but I'm still going to buy you a drink," Katie said as she eased the white van with "Divinity Florals" painted on the side of it, into a parking space.

"So are we on surveillance?"

"Yes."

"Why the hell didn't you just say so? And what's up with the baseball cap?"

"Just trying to blend in with the crowd, that's all," Katie replied as she snugged the cap down tighter on her head.

Margo looked around. "Is this one of those artsy bars?" she asked, glancing at the red door with "The Narcissus Club" emblazoned on it in purple lettering edged with gold. Margo could see crowds of people milling about inside.

"Not exactly," Katie said, getting quickly out of the van. "Come on," she said, taking Margo by the arm as they hit the street. "Consider this a date."

"A what?" Margo asked as she stopped and pulled away from Katie's grasp. Margo stood motionless and looked more intently into the window of the establishment. People sat at tables, laughing and drinking. In the center, a group of couples danced closely together. The couples were all of the same sex.

"Oh no," Margo said shaking her head, "don't even think that I'm going to …"

"Margo," Katie pleaded, "Remember Mrs. Armstrong who came in the other day? She's convinced her husband has a guy on the side. Remember how much she complimented you on your, what were they, salmon tarts? She raved about them."

"Just 'cause I can cook 'em doesn't mean …"

"It's just one night, Margo. You've done undercover work before," Katie said as she took Margo by the elbow.

Margo yanked her arm away. "First you make me dress up like a streetwalker for the Gordon case. Then you make me play a maid for the Eckert case wearing that damn getup that was meant for some skinny little white girl. Now you want me to pretend to be your girlfriend? You see any theme here, Katie? You think my people were just born to serve yours or something?"

Katie stopped. Two women who were walking arm in arm behind them parted to go around them. Katie shrugged at them and within earshot, said, "Come on, Honey, let's just go inside and have a drink and talk it over." She tugged again at Margo's arm. The two women gave her a sympathetic glance and went inside the club.

"You call me Honey one more time," Margo said yanking her arm back again, "and I'll smoke your damn hive. You got that?"

"You know you're awfully cranky lately. I'm not the only one noticing it, by the way. Besides, just think of poor Mrs. Armstrong. Her husband spends his nights e-mailing his lover rather than keeping her warm in bed. Surely you can appreciate a woman whose husband is living a double life."

"Poor my ass. She's living over in Edgerley in one of those damn McMansions. And as for my being cranky, I'm helping my friend out with the catering because he's really busy right now. I told you that. We talked about it before I took the job on. So why not just use your damn little spider technology to tap into his computer and get whatever evidence you need?"

"We have, but there's nothing like living color to convince a judge of infidelity," Katie said as she tapped the brim of the Red Sox logo on her ball cap. "This has a built in pinhole camera and is recording remotely back to the van. I just need a few shots. And here," she said reaching into her pocket, "put this on."

She pulled out a small rose-shaped brooch from her pocket and stood close to Margo as she pinned it on her sweater.

"See, now I've pinned you. We're official," Katie said grinning.

"I'm about ready to tell you where you can stick that damn pin of yours," Margo exclaimed, wagging a finger in Katie's face. "And why the hell did you have to ask me? Why couldn't you have asked Jane?"

"Can you really imagine Jane in a gay bar? Can you imagine Jane in a bar, period?"

"Okay then," Margo conceded, thinking about it, "what about the Geek Goddess?"

"You're joking, right? The woman who can't stand to be touched? She'd freak."

"But you thought I'd just fit right in ..."

"You can do this, Margo. Besides, I figured you'd understand this scene because of Marcus."

"Look, Katie, just because I have a twin brother who is gay does not mean I have some magical intuition about how to act gay. And since when do you? You been reading your Gay-to-English dictionary at night? How are you going to explain this to Captain Lughead if he finds out?"

"It's Kennedy, and Joe will understand that it's all part of the job. Just like Calvin will, if he finds out."

"Oh, no," Margo said wagging her finger again in front of Katie's face. "Let's get one thing straight right now, and by straight, I'm not talking about orientation. No one is ever to hear about this, especially Calvin. Am I damn clear about that?"

Katie grabbed the finger Margo was waving in front of her face and grinned.

"You know you're kind of cute when you get mad."

"I'm gonna kill you for this, Katie," she said as she swiped Katie's hand away.

"Besides," Katie added, "I thought we made a better couple." Margo shook her head as Katie slipped her arm back through hers. "Come on, Girlfriend. It's all in the name of work."

"You want to have to learn how to type with one hand?" Margo grumbled as Katie dragged her through the door.

"Good evening, Ladies," said the host, a young man with a buzz cut who was about the same height as Katie, as he greeted them at the door. He was wearing a white shirt and lavender vest with the club's emblem embroidered on the chest.

"Good evening," Katie said. Margo just scowled.

"Would you ladies prefer the table or the bar?"

Katie looked around the dark room. The bar was in the center of the entire room giving her a better view of the club.

"What I'd prefer," Margo began to mutter, "is to be home with my boy…" but Katie quickly pinched her on the arm.

"Ouch," Margo said grabbing her sleeve.

"Sorry," Katie said smiling at her. "The bar will be fine."

The host grabbed two menus and said, "Right this way, please."

The music was an obnoxious mix of contemporary dance tunes booming with bass so loud that Katie could feel it reverberating in her chest. She let her eyes adjust for a minute to the darkness before placing her hand in the small of Margo's back and gently pushing her forward. Margo reached back and swatted at her.

All around them, couples sat at booths and tables and eyed the two women as they passed by. Katie smiled to several, even waved to one group who all looked a bit tanked. Several people waved back. They settled in at the main bar that was in the center of the room with its heavily shellacked countertop and brass railings.

"Can I get you two something to drink?" asked a young woman with dyed pink hair and a pierced nose.

"I'll have a Smuttynose Old Brown Dog," Katie replied. "Margo?"

"Do you have a wine list?"

"Sure," the young girl said as she passed the list to Margo. Glancing quickly at the prices, Margo ordered a glass of the most expensive wine they had.

Leaning toward Katie, but loud enough for the bartender to hear, she said as sweetly as she could, "You don't mind now, Sugar, do you?"

Katie waited for the young girl to drift away out of earshot before saying, "This is not an unlimited expense account."

"Serves you damn right for tricking me into this."

"Fine, but you'll have to be the one to explain to Jane how we racked up all the liquor charges in one trip."

"I don't think so. You're the boss, remember?"

The bartender brought their glasses over and set them down in front of them.

"Where you two from?" she asked over the music. "I don't think I've ever seen you in here before."

"East Laketon," Margo announced at the exact same time Katie said, "Edgerley."

The bartender eyed them suspiciously.

"Originally, she's from East Laketon," Katie said, gesturing with her thumb. "But now we're living in Edgerley."

"I see," the young woman said, with doubt in her voice. "If you want to place an order, you can have it here or wait for an open table."

"Give us a minute," Katie said as she passed a menu to Margo and opened her own. She watched as Margo tilted the menu one way, then the other, and moved it in and out.

"Having trouble with that?" Katie asked.

"No," Margo said. "It's just the damn light in here," she said as her arm went back and forth like a trombone player's.

"Check out the daily special," Katie said. "Rub-a-Dub-Dub, Three Men in a Tub," she read. "Three spareribs rubbed with spices and served in a small bucket." Katie laughed. "Or maybe you'd prefer "Chicks With Balls," Katie continued. "Japanese Soboro chicken on a mounded ball of rice."

"I'm not eating no damn balled anything in this place," Margo muttered.

"What is that?" Margo asked pointing to a section under "Salads."

"The Green Queen," Katie read. "A hearty mix of fresh greens topped with carmelized onions, carrots and crispy chips. Mesclun for the masculine. Top with low-cal Italian dressing for the Lean Green Queen. Add zesty chipotle dressing for the Spicy Green Queen."

"If I order that, it's going to be a Mean Green Queen who's about to chew somebody's head off."

"Ah, Margo?" Katie said looking around the room. "I wouldn't be saying that in here if I were you."

The bartender returned. "Do you want to place an order?"

"I think we're all set," Katie said, returning the menus. The bartender was about to turn away when Katie stopped her, reached into the back pocket of her jeans, took out a fifty dollar bill, and laid it down on the glossy surface of the bar. The bartender moved in a bit closer.

"Look, I was hoping you might help us find someone," Katie said sliding the bill further across the heavily-lacquered wood.

"You cops?" the young woman asked eyeing them both.

"Not at all," Katie said.

"You sure?" she asked again, her pink head tilted slightly to the side like a parrot's.

Margo rolled her eyes and leaned forward toward the young girl. "Believe me, Honey, if there was a cop around here, I'd know it. The only time I didn't know it was the day I got my damn ass busted by one." She gave Katie a deliberate scowl.

"We're just trying to help out a sister in need," Katie said reassuringly. "It's a long story, but a friend asked us to check someone out. You know how it is—" Katie took out a small picture from her shirt pocket. It was cropped from the Armstrong's wedding photo and showed only George Armstrong in his black tuxedo, white rose tucked neatly into his lapel.

The bartender studied the picture for a moment then scanned the crowd, her eyes settling on a particular table in a far corner.

"Over there," she said nodding with her head.

"Is he a regular?"

"Comes around once in a while."

"Same guy?"

"Yes."

"What's your name?" Katie asked.

"Sylvia."

"Thanks, Sylvia. We appreciate the help."

Sylvia shrugged, pocketed the fifty, and turned her back to wait on other customers. Katie rose as Margo grabbed the stem of her glass and followed her.

SLOWLY, KATIE BEGAN TO work her way through the dancing crowd toward the back corner. Along the way, Margo felt a hand bump her ample behind. Margo stopped and turned to the offender, a very tall blonde woman in fishnet stockings wearing heavy makeup dressed in a tight off-the-shoulder leopard-skin-print dress who winked at her.

"How about a dance, Sweetheart?" the woman asked in a husky tone.

Margo, who was rarely at a loss for words, opened her mouth to respond, but felt Katie's arm around her waist. "Sorry, Wilma, she's with me."

"Do I know you?" the woman asked as she stared with disdain at Katie's attire.

"No, but I know you," Katie said as she whisked Margo away.

"Wilma?" Margo asked as they eased through the crowd.

"Geez, this is like taking Bambi out into the woods for the first time. Yes, Wilma. When I was working patrol, he used to hang out outside here and the Cabaret Club every night."

"You mean Wilma Flintstone is really William?"

"Yaba daba do."

KATIE AND MARGO HAD nearly maneuvered through the thick crowds toward the man's table when a loud voice rang out behind them.

"Yoo-hoo, Black Widows!"

Katie and Margo froze in their tracks.

"You have got to be kidding me," Katie murmured as she slowly turned around.

"Yoo-hoo!" they heard again.

They quickly wove their way back over toward Margo's twin brother, Marcus, and his partner, Antoine. Marcus and Antoine were co-owners of the trendy Sachet & Sashay Interior Design firm and shared office space with the Black Widow Agency.

Marcus was dressed in his trademark lavender silk shirt and wide, flowing black pants. Antoine wore gray slacks and a black sweater.

"Mother of Liza Minelli, I told you it was them," Marcus said to Antoine, who slid over in their booth to make room for the two women to join them.

"This is quite the surprise," Antoine said as he sipped at a glass of red wine.

"More than you know," Katie said.

"Well, well, well," Marcus said, eyeing her Red Sox cap and the button-down shirt. "I always told you it was just a matter of time till this one came out, but honestly, Sister," he said eyeing Margo, "I didn't think I'd ever see you in the gay-borhood."

"Don't you go getting any damn ideas in your empty head," Margo snapped back. "Believe me, this is the last place I want to be with this one," she said, nodding toward Katie.

"It's a story," Katie said as she glanced anxiously over her shoulder toward the man's corner table.

"Hey, Doll, you want to dance?" said a thirty-ish blonde-haired woman, tapping Margo on the shoulder.

Margo's eyes flared wide. "What is it with you people? You all think I can dance just because I'm black?" The woman shrugged away.

"Come on," Antoine said rising and extending his hand to Margo, "I remember how you moved those lovely hips of yours at our commitment ceremony. Let's make them all jealous."

"Oh, what the hell," Margo said as she set her glass of wine down. "Just one and only because I know at least you won't be hitting on me."

"You never know," Antoine teased.

"Why does everyone keep asking her?" Katie said frowning as she sat down next to Marcus and watched Margo and Antoine pick up the rhythm of the music. "I can dance, too, you know," she said watching Margo and Antoine.

Marcus rolled his eyes. "No offense, Katarina Darling, but I've seen cardboard that wasn't as stiff as you."

Katie waved him away with her hand and gestured for a refill.

"And by the way," he said looking up and down her outfit, "where in heaven's name did you get that loathsome getup? Were they having a closeout sale at Debutchery?"

"I'm just trying to blend in," Katie replied sharply.

"Look around, Wonder Woman. Do you see any of these lovely ladies dressed like they just got hit by the transsexual bus?"

Katie looked and realized that most of the women were, in fact, very nicely dressed.

Katie shrugged. "Whatever. Seems I'm out of fashion no matter where I am."

"You can say that again," Marcus mumbled.

Katie leaned forward and sniffed at Marcus' drink. "What's that you're drinking?"

Marcus took a slow sip from the highball glass before answering. "It's a delicioso blend of Gin, Peach Schnapps, Vodka, Rum, and Tequila."

"And it's called?"

Marcus raised his glass to his lips and flashed his eyes. "A ManEater."

"Why am I not surprised?"

"So pray, Katarina, do tell why you're here? Have you finally decided to come to the dark side?"

"Very funny, Marcus, but we're actually working undercover. At least we were undercover until someone started shouting at us from across the room."

"Forgive me for trying to be social."

Margo and Antoine returned to the table grinning.

"Here's to a fine dancer," Margo said raising her glass to Antoine. "My brother doesn't deserve a classy man like you."

"I keep telling him that," Antoine replied, his warm brown eyes twinkling. They clinked glasses.

"They're working undercover," Marcus announced loudly to Antoine just as the waitress brought Katie another Smuttynose. The waitress gave Katie and Margo a suspicious look.

"Why don't you just ask the DJ to announce that?" Katie complained.

"Don't need to in that outfit," Marcus quipped back. "And by the way, since when does your little spider firm take on investi-*gay*-tions? I thought your clients were all straight as pine boards and by pine boards, I do mean white pine."

"For your information," Katie said, "The Black Widow Agency does not care about the color nor the sexual orientation of its clients as long as those clients are in need of assistance. And in this particular case, this client believes her husband is two-timing her with another man."

Marcus whistled. "Don't get your baseball cap all twisted up in a knot. I was merely asking why you were here."

"We're here because of him," Katie said gesturing over her shoulder toward the back corner table. "His wife would like to know why he's lost interest, if you catch my drift."

"Like a flat rainbow sail on a windy day," Marcus said.

"Is there anything we can do to help?" Antoine asked kindly.

Marcus quickly put his hand on his partner's arm. "Antoine, my beloved, I don't think it's appropriate for us to offer them help."

"And why is that, Marcus?" Katie asked.

"If the gentleman in question in more interested in exploring his true calling, I don't think we should interfere. It's the gay Code of Ethics."

"Gay Code of Ethics, my ass," Margo said. "We're not on him, no pun intended, because he's gay. We want his sorry ass because he's cheating on his wife. He can explain his change of heart to the judge when he's handing over the damn keys to the million-dollar house."

"Still," Marcus protested, "if he loses the homo sweet homo, that's his problem. I just don't think we should be interfering with Mother Nature."

"I'll tell you what damn mother is interfering...," Margo began.

"Margo! Katie said. "Okay, we respect your feelings and your spirituality," Katie said a little too politely, "but we're on the job and a client is paying us to get our work done, so if you'll excuse us. Come on, Margo," she said, gulping at her beer and grabbing Margo under the arm. "Let's go mingle. See you boys around the shop," she called over her shoulder.

DESPITE MANY PROTESTATIONS, MARGO finally agreed to dance with Katie. She shook her head at Katie's stiff movements. Katie kept her body facing George Armstrong. Just as she saw him reach across and take the younger man's hand in his, the music abruptly changed to a slow dance. She grabbed Margo and pulled her close.

"What the hell?" Margo asked, as she tried to pull back.

"Work with me," Katie said as she pulled her tighter. "Trust me, this will nail his ass to the wall."

"May I remind you that we're in a gay bar? I wouldn't be going around talking about anyone's ass being nailed anywhere. And keep your damn hands above the waist."

"Nice perfume," Katie teased as she nestled her chin on the top of Margo's head and swayed back and forth.

Just as the song stopped, the younger man reached across the table and kissed George Armstrong on the lips.

"Bingo," Katie said as she pulled away. "That's a wrap."

"Damn right it is. Next thing you know you'll be announcing our damn engagement."

She and Margo began to thread their way back through the crowd. "How about we head on back to my place for a few drinks?" Katie shouted above the music.

"You just don't take a hint, do you? You're not my type."

"Aw come on," Katie said. "I'm serious. Let's head back to my place for a nightcap. We never get to just hangout and talk."

"I've had enough of you for one day, thank you," Margo shouted above the music.

"Is she bothering you?" a deep voice rang out. Margo stopped dead as Wilma strategically placed herself between Katie and Margo.

"What?" Katie said feigning a laugh. "Hey, I was just kidding. She's not even … We're not even … Look, it's okay," Katie said, but Wilma was not budging. Margo tried to get around her, but Wilma boxed her in.

"Doesn't sound like you treat your girl very nice."

"I … she's … Are you kidding? We get along fine," Katie said as reassuringly as she could. "Tell him … her …" Katie said imploringly to Margo, who stood behind Wilma with her mouth gaping open.

"Then how 'bout you prove it by kissing and making up?"

Katie gulped. "We're fine, really. If you'll just let us go …"

"I said to kiss and make up," Wilma said more firmly. "You got a problem with that?"

"Yes. No. I mean we're not …"

THE COMMOTION CAUSED A small crowd to gather around them. Before they knew what was happening, Katie and Margo were surrounded by a group that was getting bigger by the minute, as the regulars wondered what had rankled Wilma so.

"There seems to be a big misunderstanding," Katie said. "I was just joking around. Ask her."

"I said to kiss and make up."

Wilma shoved Margo into Katie as the crowd began to chant, "Kiss her, kiss her."

Margo's eyes bore into Katie's as Katie shrugged and said, "I'm not sure we have a choice right now…"

"No way."

"You see these people?" Katie asked. "They're not very happy with me. They didn't call it the Gay Revolution for nothing."

"It's your problem if they're all having a fit, Katie, not mine."

"Yes, but unfortunately, it's a fit for a queen, or in this case, quite a few angry ones."

"Kiss her!" the crowd demanded.

"I don't think so."

"Fine," Katie relented. "Name your price."

Margo looked around at the crowd as it grew more animated.

"I want a week's paid vacation so I can help my friend out with the catering during the day and get some sleep," Margo declared.

"That would be double-dipping."

"And I need a new refrigerator. Mine is worn out and barely keeps the food cold."

"Kiss her! Kiss her!" the crowd chanted behind them.

"Now you're pushing it."

"You want me to make nice-nice or do you want this to be a new episode on Gays of Our Lives—The Revolution?"

Katie glanced around at the throng of people surrounding them, who were growing more and more impatient by the minute. "I see your point."

"Stainless steel."

"Pucker up," Katie said as she closed her eyes and leaned forward. Just as Margo leaned toward her, they both heard, "Mother of Mercy!" shouted from the crowd.

"Heaven's to Britney Spears, what is going on here?" Marcus said as he broke through and quieted down the crowd.

"This one's been giving her girl a hard time, Marcus," Wilma replied. "I just want to make sure they're cool before they leave."

"Oh for Mercy's sakes," Marcus said as he pushed through and grabbed Katie by the arm. "This is one of your own."

Wilma eyed Katie suspiciously. "Are you sure, Marcus?"

"Abs and pecs-solutely! He and I have dropped our letters into the same box a few times. Granted the ensemble is atrocious, but that's because of other issues," Marcus said as he made a circling gesture around his head. "Everything else is still intact. Do you think any real woman would ever dare to be seen in public with that ..." he said wagging a finger up and down at Katie, "... fashion homicide?"

"That explains it," Wilma said, eyeing Katie suspiciously.

"Inexcusable," Marcus continued. "Now come over to my table and Antoine and I will buy you a delicious cocktail. What a lovely print, Darling," Marcus said as he put his arm through Wilma's. "Leopard is the new black, you know. You wear it so well. And I'm loving the off-the-shoulder look. You can carry it with those broad boards you have." Marcus glanced back over his shoulder and mouthed "Leave," to Katie and Margo who were more than willing to listen to him for once.

ABOUT THE AUTHOR

Felicia Donovan is a recognized expert in the field of law enforcement technology, and currently works at a New England-based police department as a civilian Information Systems manager. She swears by the adage, "every keystroke is recoverable," and has worked on the forensic recovery of files and data from computers used in crimes. She is also renowned for her ability to digitally enhance photographs and has assisted the FBI on cases related to digital photography, as well as providing technical advice relative to cyber crimes.

She is the founder of CLEAT (Communication, Law Enforcement and Technology), an organization comprised of law enforcement professionals around the New England region, and is a member of the International Association of Chiefs of Police and the New Hampshire Police Association.

Donovan lives in New Hampshire with her two children who don't shed, and three dogs that do.